SCORPIO

ZODIAC KILLERS #12

WL KNIGHTLY

BRIXBAXTER PUBLISHING

Scorpio
Zodiac Killers #12

Copyright © 2018 by WL Knightly

First Edition.

Editor: Eric Martinez
Cover Art: Kellie Dennis at Book Cover by Design

CHAPTER 1

BAY

Numb.

That was how Bay felt about Mia's disappearance. His reaction might seem odd to others, but feeling nothing was safer than allowing his white-hot rage to bubble up to the surface. Anytime he thought about how they might find Mia, his fury threatened to explode like an erupting volcano.

Bay pushed it down. Anger was a gift, a tool to be used, but only at the right moment. He would save those emotions and unleash them when it was time for violence. Mia's killer would suffer.

It wasn't a question of her being alive at that point. The asshole, Max, had taken her from him once just for fun— just to say fuck you —but now Bay knew he had taken her for good.

Staring at Mia's pink bedroom walls didn't help. He had been so annoyed at her for the spilled paint and the tiny droplets of splatter she'd managed to get here and there. No longer could he scold her or put her over his knee for a spanking. No longer would he see the defiant gleam in her eye or get hard from how much it turned him on.

No, the other player in this deadly game had made a decisive move, and Bay was trapped in a corner, unable to do a damned thing about it.

Bay didn't like being cornered. There was only one way to win from that position, and that was to murder every fucking obstacle in his way, including his nemesis. One way or another, Officer Max would burn, even if Bay had to drag him down to Hell himself.

He kicked one of Mia's sparkly unicorns across the room where the stuffed fucker bounced off the wall. "Fuck!"

Footsteps approached behind him, and he collected himself. Lane Simon walked into the room, looking like the shell of a man. He had been staying at Bay's house out of precaution. It seemed safer than anywhere else.

"Any word?" Lane asked. He looked around the room and rocked on his heels.

Bay knew the two men looked out of place in the glittery pink palace that Mia had made her own. He took a deep breath and walked over to get the unicorn from across the room. "No. Not a damned thing. I got kicked out of the police station by our lovely friend, Detective Blake, and I've been here ever since." He picked up the stuffed creature and put it on Mia's bed.

Lane gave him a sappy look. "It's okay to let it out, man. I keep having moments. I can't believe that Nona is gone. At least you have hope."

Bay shook his head. "If you think that, then you're a fool."

He turned and sat on the bed which was like an ocean of pink ruffles. The bedding still smelled like her.

"Call me a fool all you want," Lane said. "But there's a chance she could be alive. You don't know what he's done with her, but I *do* know what he's done with Nona. She's never coming back from what he did to her, so I wish I had the option of *hope*."

The man walked to the window, turning his back on Bay. Lane's hand went to his face, and Bay knew he was wiping away tears. Bay refused to waste his time with such weakness. Tears would not buy back the time he would miss with Mia, and they couldn't prevent the pain her death would cause Lila and their mother when they found out.

But Lane was still so much like that whipped kid from back in the day. He'd never built up walls around his heart, so he still felt the sharp sting of every emotion.

Bay decided to take it easy on him. "Look, I know you're hurting, and I'm sorry about Nona, but false hope will get me nowhere. We need to figure out how to make him pay for Nona. For this." He took his phone out of his pocket and turned it on. The image of Lou's pale face shone on the screen. "And for what he's done with Mia."

Bay had gone out looking for Lou on his way home. He found Lou's car, which had been robbed, probably by some homeless people down at the river where Max had abandoned it. Bay had called the cops anonymously. It was all he could do for the old man who had been a loyal employee and friend since he was a kid.

Lane walked across the room to the door. "I think you should let the cops handle it for now."

Bay knew better. "So, let Darek handle it, you mean? And what's Darek going to do when Officer Asshole tells everyone why he's been killing people? That it's because when we were all kids, we fucked up and killed a girl and the cops pinned it on his dad. Darek is going to piss his pants and pass out. That's what he's going to do."

Lane gave him a hard look. "I just mean for the time being. I want to nail this asshole just like you do, but I'm going to be smart about it."

Bay shook his head. "Smart would have been taking him out when I had the chance, but you and Darek made me wait. Now, look where we're at. I'm going to have to figure out how to get to him behind bars, and with him being a cop, my connections in general population aren't going to be any help." If the other remaining Zodiacs hadn't pussed out on him, he wouldn't be in this situation.

Lane leaned against the doorjamb. "So, there's no way to get to him, and—"

"I didn't say there's no way to get to him, Lane." Bay got to his feet. "It's just going to take a little longer. I have to figure out which guard is the most desperate for a big payday."

"Jesus, Bay. Are you even listening to yourself? You're supposed to uphold the law. Do you even have any respect for your position as an attorney? Now you're going to pay some hard-up guard to do your dirty work?"

Bay shrugged. "They won't have to do anything but turn their back or arrange for my guys on the inside to be where I need them. Not all of us are the teacher's pet, Lane. I work within and around the law when necessary. I use what I know to my advantage, and before you give me another look of shock, don't pretend I'm the only one." Lane might not be crooked himself, but he wasn't perfect either. "I'm going to find someone who can get to him."

"You better make sure that you don't get busted trying to set that up," Lane said. "Max is a cop, and a well-liked one. He was even good enough to be Darek's best friend for years."

"Let's not give him too much credit," Bay said. "He's not exactly the hardest person to fool."

Darek had been one of the easier Zodiacs to lure into his web, and all because his daddy didn't like him. He had often wondered if he should have found another Sagittarius, but then, he could have said the same for the others. He had not chosen them for their bravery, but because of how malleable they were.

Lane took a deep breath. "Darek's done a good job so far, keeping us out of jail. I don't think he can save your ass if you get caught trying to bribe a prison guard."

"Darek is handling something for me," Bay said. "He's talking to Marvin. I didn't know what the man might say, so I suggested that he be the one to question him. I'd been a little lax by allowing Mia to be around and privy to my business. Since I have no idea what she and her little gossiping boyfriend discussed, I thought it best."

"I never told Nona anything," Lane said. "She had no idea I had a past before her. She was so self-centered. She never asked about me, and it wasn't like I could have told her anything about the Zodiacs."

"It's a secret society, Lane, or I guess I should say it *was*." There weren't enough of them left to consider it a society anymore, and once Max ran his mouth, the "secret" part would be gone too. "You're not supposed to tell her anything. Mia used to be clueless, and I remained fairly confident that she didn't care anything about what was going on."

"Do you think the others really didn't tell their spouses or confidants?" Lane asked, frowning.

Bay shrugged. "Someone told the killer enough, and even though he denied it, I think Justin told his little online girlfriend too much. Since we know that Max must have been the man in the shadow with the first victim, then I guess that theory is right."

"I plan on staying in town," said Lane, changing the subject. "At least until I take care of Nona's belongings and funeral arrangements. I know her aunt is beside herself, and she's too old to travel. I told her I'd take care of everything."

"Fuck," said Bay. He hadn't let himself think about any of that. There was still so much to do: arrangements to make, people to inform, a killer to kill. "I forgot I'll have to figure out what to do with Mia's remains. If they ever find her."

"I'm having Nona cremated," Lane said. "She wouldn't want anyone to see her that way. You know, dead. She used to get so upset when we'd go anywhere. 'Does my hair look okay? Is my lipstick too dark? Does this make my ass look big?' She was the most insecure model I've ever met, but then I guess all women are like that, aren't they?"

Bay smiled. "Not my Mia. She had confidence. She held her head up from the moment I met her. I think that's why I loved her so much." Bay let out a long breath. His love wasn't the same as everyone else's, he supposed, but in his own way, he knew he did truly love the girl.

He didn't even mind the sappy word "love." Mia had earned it. He was glad that he had said it to her at least once, and funnily enough, he had been telling her how he'd always provide for her, even after he was gone. She'd admitted loving him too. At the time, it hadn't sunk in, but it meant a lot to him that someone as amazing as her gave a shit.

Now she was gone, and all of the provisions he'd made for her would fall to either his child or to her sister. Everything would have to be changed now.

Lane glanced around the living room. "I didn't know if I should stay here, or if I should just crash at Nona's. Now that they've caught Max, I guess it's safe."

"You don't have to leave. You can come and go as you please. Just make sure you don't forget the security codes." It took two to get into Bay's private estate these days.

Lane nodded. "I might. I guess it depends on how I feel. As soon as Darek's girl calls me down to the station, I'm going to have to deliver the lie of a lifetime and tell her that pedo ring story we made up."

He had a lost look in his eyes, and Bay couldn't help but be grateful that he didn't let things like this turn him into a weeping weakling.

Lane looked up and sighed. "Sue me for mourning someone I care about and not wanting to be known as a victim," he said. "I can see it in your eyes that you think I'm ridiculous for crying. It doesn't make me weak."

"I never said that." *But I certainly think it.* "Deal with your grief your way. I just don't know how to feel the same, okay? I'm not good with this kind of shit."

"Hey, we're both hurting and heartbroken," said Lane. "It's okay, really. I won't judge you for dealing with your emotions. I know you have them, Bay. You might not think it, but you do."

"I'm not hurt or heartbroken. I'm pissed off. And as for dealing with my emotions? All I have to say is, the longer I have to wonder where she is, the more I'm going to make it hurt when I make Max pay for what he did."

CHAPTER 2

DAREK

With Lizzy was still in the thick of the investigation with her blinders on, Darek knew he had to take the opportunity to go and interview Marvin, who was more than willing to talk, even though he was stuck in a hospital bed.

Darek walked down the hallway of the hospital, where the walls were still an ugly shade of mauve left over from the last remodel back in the early nineties. He couldn't help but think how the case had taken such a dramatic turn. Not only had Nona been brutally slaughtered, but Mia was unaccounted for after a vicious attack that left Marvin stabbed.

Now, what they thought was the murder weapon was in the forensic team's hands, and Darek knew there was no way Max would get away with what he'd done. Darek's biggest concern was wondering what Max would say in his defense. Would he reveal that this was a revenge mission, designed to pay them back for what they'd done to his father and Emily Johnson? Or would he keep his promise to keep quiet? Every moment Darek walked around as a free man, he couldn't help but wonder when it was all going to come crashing down.

What would that do to him and Lizzy? She would never be with him if she knew his dark past, and she would certainly never forgive him for what he'd done to the investigation. Not only would his life be over, but his career and his freedom would be gone as well.

It would be such a waste. They had been working so solidly together since Noah identified Max, and now, Darek's ex-partner was a big powder keg, ready to blow. He only hoped that Bay would make good on his word and figure out how to take Max out behind bars before he ran his mouth. The sinking feeling in Darek's gut wasn't going anywhere, anytime soon, and he was sure to come out of this with an ulcer if he survived at all.

He turned the corner to Marvin's room, and when he approached, he found the door closed, and quiet voices spoke on the other side. Darek knocked softly.

"Come in," said Marvin, whose voice was strong, but feminine. When Darek peeked around the door into the room, Marvin's eyes widened. "Hello, Detective." It was as if he didn't expect to see someone so close to Bay come to talk to him, but Darek wouldn't have let anyone else handle this.

"How are you holding up?" asked Darek. He looked over at Marvin's friend, a woman he'd seen at the fashion show. Her purple hair made her memorable. She gave a weak smile and shifted in her seat uncomfortably.

"I'd be better if you're here to tell me you found Mia alive, and that asshole who did this is behind bars." Marvin's eyes were weary, but that was what Darek expected from a man who'd been so close to death.

"I can tell you he's locked up, but as for Mia, I'm sorry. We still haven't found her. That's why I'm here. To find out if you remember anything now that it's all had a little time to sink in."

Marvin turned his head so Darek could see the bruise. "Do you think it's sunk in?"

"Wow, you took a hell of a hit." He looked over at the woman again, and this time, she got up out of her seat.

"I'm going to go downstairs," she said. "Text me when you're done?" She gave Marvin a hopeful look. "Can I get you anything?"

Marvin smiled. "A coffee would be nice. Something with flavor, not this black shit they keep trying to pass off." He turned his nose up and looked to Darek as she disappeared out the door.

"So, was it Max?" Marvin's voice was so rough, it sounded like he'd gargled a bag of rocks.

Darek nodded. "I guess you've heard all about him from Mia."

Marvin shrugged. "A little. She and I had gotten close. I know you and Bay are friends."

"Friends is a loose term for what we are. Some people are just stuck together by circumstance. But I guess if that's the only label that fits, then yeah, we are." Darek never thought he'd have to admit that to anyone, and he had a feeling Bay would disagree. Bay didn't care much for friends. He preferred puppets.

"I don't think it's a coincidence that it's you who showed up to talk to me," Marvin said.

Darek held up his hands. "Hey, I'm just here doing my job." He walked over and took a seat where the woman had been.

"If you say so, Detective. They could have sent any other officer to hear what I have to say, but I get the lead detective on the hottest case of the year."

"Well, it *is* my case," Darek said. Still, he had to give Marvin credit. "You're a smart man. So, why don't you just tell me what happened with Mia? I need to know everything you can remember."

Marvin exhaled a long breath. "We were painting at her boutique like we had been planning for days. I got involved because I had recently quit my job at Dos and decided to start fresh with Mia. I liked her style, and I wanted to sink my creative teeth into something new and fresh. I wanted to be in on the birth of a great brand, and I knew I could bring in my expertise. Even if it meant starting from the ground up and taking up a paint roller for the first time in fifteen years."

"You put a lot on the line, changing careers to work for her," Darek said.

"Well, before you make me sound too heroic, it wasn't all about the rebirth of my creativity. It was no secret that Bay Collins was about to throw some serious money my way for my work, and his pockets run deep." He shrugged and held up a perfectly manicured, pointed, polished nail, complete with sparkling crystals. "Don't get me wrong. I did it for Mia. She's a little diamond in an otherwise ugly situation, but I could look past all of that because I knew she could really shine."

Darek wondered what Mia's life was really like with Bay Collins. "Ugly situation? Did she tell you things about her life? Was she mistreated?"

"Well, call me old-fashioned, but being in an open sexual relationship with your pregnant sister's husband is an ugly situation. I guess some find it acceptable these days, but to me, that's some scandalous shit."

Darek grinned. "That's one way to put it."

"I didn't have the heart to tell Mia." Marvin shrugged. "To each their own, I guess. Who was I to let morals knock me out of a great job?"

"It is a bit disturbing." Darek wasn't one to get into Bay's business, but he often felt horrible for Lila, who had to live in seclusion like she was carrying the fucking Anti-Christ.

"More than a bit. I hear the sister doesn't know and she's treated like a surrogate. It's the only thing about Mia I can say I don't like. She is well programmed when it comes to her man."

"Well programmed is right," Darek said.

"She's treated like a pet, and the poor thing just doesn't see it. I wonder at times if Bay has any affection for the poor girl at all, or if he simply sees her as a project. Kind of like Mia's shop was hers; she was his. Only he painted her walls with lavish clothes and handbags."

Darek didn't want to rush Marvin, but he also didn't need to psychoanalyze Bay and Mia's relationship. "So, what happened the day you were attacked?"

"Bay came in to see the place, and he got a phone call about Nona Pace. Elena told me what happened to her. She was one of my friends, and I guess somehow, he knew her too. She dated a friend of yours?" His sculpted brows rose with the question.

"Yes. Nona was murdered. Max killed her, and he's been arrested. We're sure that he's the one who attacked you and took Mia."

Marvin's eyes widened. "There's too many people dying. It's such a waste. Nona was a good girl." He paused a moment, and Darek was patient enough to give him time. "So at the shop, Bay told us to order a pizza and sit tight. He was afraid that something would happen to Mia. He left, and we did what he said. Mia knew he'd lose his shit if she went against his wishes. I asked her if Bay had ever hit her, and she said no, but she was terrified of him. He's crazy, that one."

Darek didn't mean to nod in agreement, but Marvin gave a knowing look when he did.

"You must know how he is," Marvin said. "We went back to work after ordering the pizza, and Mia had opened up the back door to let in some air. The paint fumes had our taste buds fucked up, and Mia said she wanted to taste the fucking pizza when it got there. I had gone around to the front side to start working on the second coat. I heard Mia scream and thought she probably stepped in paint again. She was messy and a bit overdramatic." He took another deep breath. "I didn't even make it around the corner. Something hit me in the side of my head. I went down and then felt the heat of the knife going in me."

"You were stabbed after you were struck? After you'd gone down?" Darek couldn't help but think it was strange.

Max nodded. "The asshole had already taken me down, but I guess he had to make a fucking point so Mia wouldn't fight or something. I don't know. I was out of it. I came to when I heard Bay and his friend show, but I had lost so much blood. Luckily, the wound didn't hit anything important. I'm told I'm a very lucky man. Can you believe that? For once, I'm lucky, and that's how it has to be. Lucky I didn't die? I'd rather win the fucking lottery, thank you." He raked his long nails through his hair and turned his nose up to the air.

Darek gave a half-hearted smile. The poor guy had been through hell. "But you never saw who stabbed you? Who hit you?" He wasn't going to be able to pin this one on Max unless there was other evidence. The officers had been working the scene, but there wasn't much to collect. Max had been smart enough to not leave anything behind.

Marvin shook his head. "I wish I could say yes, but I didn't. If I can help in any other way, please let me know."

"Just focus on getting better." Darek got to his feet.

"How can I when Mia's out there somewhere? What are the chances she's found alive? That asshole thought nothing of stabbing me, and I wasn't even his target. He wanted Mia."

"Did she tell you anything about Max?" Darek asked. "She had a relationship with him, you know?"

He got an uncomfortable look in his eye. "She told me things, all right. You can bet he was a real freak if she ran back to Bay. He used to meet her at a motel, and then he'd blindfold her and do all sorts of shit to her. She never really got too into it, and she said she never told Bay. He once put her in a trunk."

"What?" Darek asked. "Did she say why?"

Marvin got a blank look on his face. "Shit. She never told me. She just said it kept getting more and more odd. He wanted her to explore some dark shit, and she wasn't into it. She thought he was a nice guy, but she said she had just gotten out of that kind of thing, and she needed time to think about what she was going to do. She decided in the end—get this—that no one could truly love her as much as Bay because he was family. So, she went back to him." Marvin rolled his eyes. "Talk about taboo. She's a little warped, but I suspect it's because she doesn't know anything else. She'd talk to me about her and Bay like it was nothing. I guess after a while, even I became used to it."

"Thanks, Marvin." Darek offered the man his hand, and they shook. "I'll keep you informed. If you think of anything else, something Mia might have told you, just call me."

"Yeah, sure thing. I won't talk to anyone else. You don't have to worry about that."

Darek smiled and left the room, believing that Marvin knew when to put up and when to shut up.

CHAPTER 3

LANE

With everything going on, Lane thought that nothing could make him feel any worse. Until Special Agent McNamara, who he had only known as Darek's latest love interest, had called him from the FBI and asked him to come into the NYPD station and give his statement.

She had suspicions about the Zodiacs' connection, and because of that, he, along with Bay and Darek, had devised a quick plan, one that would surely do the trick but tarnish his reputation in the process.

He had spent his entire life trying not to be a victim, and the plan would make him appear as such. It would also haunt him forever, along with making him a hypocrite and liar.

As he drove to the station, his phone rang from the seat beside him. He hit the blue tooth feature on his rental car. "Hello?"

"Hey, it's me," said Bay. "I was just checking in at the office, and it seems we've had a message come through while we were busy dealing with our girlfriend drama."

Lane tried not to get riled up about Bay's nonchalant phrasing. He had already accepted that Bay was a heartless asshole. "Yeah? Is it from Kenneth Warner?"

"Yes, it says that Otis's sons' names were Otis Jr. and Maxwell

Gough. I'm assuming Smith is his alias. Fucker couldn't be bothered to be a bit more creative."

"Well, too bad it won't change what I have to do," Lane said. "I've been called down to the station for questioning. I feel like I'm going to throw up. I've never been so fucking eaten up with nerves in my life." He had been shaking all morning. It reminded him of how it felt to go to school when he was being bullied daily and how it felt to be on that floor with Huck's shoe in his back as the piss permeated his pores.

"Just stick to the story, and let it all play out," Bay said. "It'll be fine. Just tell them that you never knew there were others, that Gough had lured you into the woods, branded you in some weird marking ceremony. You don't have to get too detailed. Let that bitch fill in some of the blanks."

Lane nodded. "It should work out just like I said. They'll have their excuse, and I'll look innocent. It will be a dead man's word against my own."

"Make sure if they mention what happened with the girl, that you tell them you didn't know anything about that. And you didn't know the other guys very well. You're a victim. They aren't going to want to tear you apart." Bay's tone was demanding, and it didn't do anything to calm Lane's nerves.

"Yeah, I hear you. I'll handle it." He couldn't help but sound sour, with bile stinging the back of his throat.

Bay let out a sigh. "Hey, it's all going to be over soon. You'll see."

Lane thought it was easy for him to say. "What if Max catches wind, and it triggers him to talk?"

"I'm going to take him out before he has a chance. I'm working on it, but meanwhile, Darek will handle it."

Bay made it all sound so simple, but he wasn't the one everyone would look at like some kind of pathetic, weak man who couldn't speak up and stop what was going on.

"Yeah, look. I'm here." He turned into the parking lot. "I'll have to call you back when I'm done."

"Yeah, let me know how it goes." Bay hung up the phone without a goodbye.

Lane put the phone down and pulled into a parking space. He sat there a minute before getting out of the car, trying to steady his nerves. He knew what he had to do, and he wasn't nervous about the story, just his delivery. He'd never been the kind of person who could lie. He'd always hated defending people who couldn't tell the truth to save their lives, and this made him feel like everyone would see right through him.

He got out of the car, and by the time he went inside, Darek was waiting for him. "Hey, I hoped you'd come right over. I wanted to talk to you a minute before Lizzy comes down."

"Yeah, I just got off the phone with Bay," Lane said. "Max's real name is Maxwell Gough. He's the other son, just like we thought, so this story is going to set him off. I'm not sure if it's the right thing to do after all."

"Right or wrong, it's all we've got, and we don't have to tell everyone right away. I'll talk to Lizzy and make sure this doesn't get out." About that time, Darek looked up and saw Lizzy coming up the hall. "There she is now." As Lizzy approached, Darek's demeanor changed. He hiked up his pants and stood a little taller. "I was just about to find you."

"Thank you for coming in, Mr. Simon," she said. "Let's take this down the hall."

She gave Darek a pointed look and then turned to lead the way. Darek followed along behind her, and Lane couldn't help but wonder how they made their relationship work in this atmosphere. Lizzy was so formal, even though she'd already met Lane at the fashion event. He imagined it was the same way she was with Darek: warm and fuzzy when they were alone, and cold as a snake when they were at work.

She walked into a room with a long table. "Let's all have a seat. Could I get you anything? Soda? Coffee? Water?"

He felt like he was about to be interrogated because of how eager she was to make him comfortable. He wondered if she'd try and blame him for what had happened in some strange attempt to get her policeman friend off.

15

"No thanks," he said, his mind still reeling.

"All right," said Lizzy. "Then we'll begin." She placed a recorder on the table. "I do have to tell you that this is being recorded for your protection and ours. Please state your name."

"Lane Simon."

"I am Special Agent McNamara, and this is my partner on this case, Detective Darek Blake. Could you please tell me about when you first discovered Ms. Nona Pace was deceased?"

"I had gotten a call from her to come by and pick up some of my things," Lane said. "I live in New Orleans, and I was hoping to go back home. I'd come up to stay with Nona for her fashion show, to offer some support."

Lizzy kept her head down and scribbled on a piece of paper. "The fashion show where Ethan Cline was murdered. And you were a friend of his, were you not?"

"Yeah, I knew Ethan."

"And is his death the reason you're still in town?" she asked.

"No, I was just spending a little more time with Nona." He wasn't about to give himself a stronger connection to Ethan, and with his funeral in Tennessee, it made no sense to say he'd stayed for the services.

"So, were you staying somewhere else?" Lizzy asked. "Why would Ms. Pace have to call you to come over?"

Lane let out a long breath. "We had an argument the day before. She wanted to get married, but I felt that she—well, it's going to sound weird, but you just had to know Nona. I felt like the only reason she wanted to get married was because her two best friends had recently gotten engaged. I want to be married because I'm in love, not because it's what others are doing. I had left the night before and stayed with a friend. When I showed up at her place, I saw her car outside. She wouldn't come to the door. I heard her music on, so I went inside. After some searching, I gave up looking for her. I thought she'd stepped out. But then I found her in the closet when I went to gather my things." He closed his eyes and could still see her there.

"And do you know why she'd be marked up with the zodiac?" Lizzy asked.

Lane shook his head.

"Do you know why she would be treated exactly like another young woman, years ago? Have you ever been to Virginia, Mr. Simon?"

Lane glanced over to Darek, who looked away. He had to answer the questions. It was the only way to deflect that authorities from the truth. "I have been to Virginia. When I was a child. I went to camp there."

"I see," Lizzy said. "And what was the name of that camp?"

"Camp Victory," he said. "It was a summer camp for boys. I spent a couple of years there."

"And you knew Ethan Cline from that camp, didn't you?" she asked.

He looked at Darek, who was still looking down at the papers in front of Lizzy.

"I did. We were acquaintances."

"Do you know a man named Otis Gough? He was convicted of a murder years ago. The brutal murder of a girl named Emily Johnson."

Lane shrugged. "I don't know her."

Lizzy took a deep breath. "But you know of her murder, don't you?"

Lane nodded. "I know that Otis Gough was sent away for the murder of a young girl. I didn't know her name."

Darek cleared his throat. "Did you know Mr. Gough?"

Lane knew it was time for their cover story. "I did."

Lizzy's eyes lit with surprise. "You did? And how did you know him?"

What Lane had to say wasn't easy, and he realized that it added to the effect. "He was known to hang around the woods near our camp."

The agent's eyes narrowed. "Is that a fact? And did you approach him? Talk to him?" There was an accusing tone in her voice, and it struck Lane the wrong way.

"He approached *me*. He seemed okay at first, but I had no reason to

17

fear anyone. He called me away from the edge of camp one day. Told me that he'd trapped a rabbit, and if I wanted, he'd give me one of its feet for luck. I thought it would be something cool to have. That the others would be jealous when I made a keyring out of it. I followed him into the woods."

"Did anyone notice you missing?" Darek asked.

Lane shook his head. "No, the counselors were all in bed. I had gotten up to go the bathroom. He liked to linger around there. We didn't think anything of it. I really thought the other adults knew him, but when I went with him that night..." He paused, the words not wanting to come from his lips.

Darek leaned forward. "Did he really have a rabbit?"

"No," said Lane. "He didn't have a rabbit. He brought me out to a campfire, said to wait while he went to get the rabbit, that I could help him cook it. I sat there a while, and he came back without it. Said a dog must have gotten it. I had no reason not to believe him. He said he wanted to make it up to me. He had a lot of tattoos and asked if I wanted one. I said I wasn't sure. He assured me that he could give me one, and it wouldn't hurt. He made me take off my shirt."

"And he branded you?" asked Lizzy, who covered her mouth.

"Yeah." Lane took a deep breath.

"And then what happened?" asked Darek.

"He touched me. I never told anyone. I still don't like talking about it."

Lizzy moved to the edge of her seat. "What? Otis Gough *abused* you?"

"He said that my mark made me his, that I was forever bound in his secret society. I was so scared." He didn't know what else to say and figured that silence was best.

Darek shook his head. "So, Otis Gough was tied into child porn? Go figure. I guess that explains how Tad Halston was connected."

Lane looked up at Darek. "I don't want my name brought into any of this. I'm a business owner, and I have a life that could be disrupted."

Darek nodded. "Don't worry. We'll keep this information under our hat for as long as we can. We have a lot of investigating to do, and neither one of us want the press on this."

Lizzy nodded in agreement. "Yeah, there's no need to make any moves just yet. I'm sorry for what happened to you. I guess Gough was guilty after all."

"Yeah." Lane felt the disappointment in himself burning inside. "I'd appreciate the discretion. I'm not speaking to the press or anyone else about this. It was a long time ago."

"Thank you, Mr. Simon. That will help us immensely. We'll be in touch." Lizzy seemed satisfied, and that was all he could ask for.

"I'll walk you out," said Darek, getting to his feet. He and Lane walked together as they went to the parking lot.

"What did I just do?" asked Lane, walking to his rental car. "Remind me why I just lied to your girlfriend."

Darek's hand fell on his shoulder. "To save my ass. I can tell her that I didn't know any of that shit. With you being a lawyer, it's not out of the ordinary that I met you or Bay. I'll be able to pacify her until we can get rid of Max. So, thanks for that."

"For the record, I feel like a piece of shit," he said, opening up his car door. Not even Darek had a response for that one. Instead, he gave Lane a sympathetic look. Lane could imagine he felt the same way.

CHAPTER 4

BAY

Bay walked into the busy police station, expecting someone to tackle him to the floor or tell him to get out. He didn't exactly storm into the place, but he had definitely walked in with as much purpose as the last time.

He was met by the usual sea of blue. Officers lingered around between their shifts, and the ones who were destined to be behind their desks were scarce. Bay suspected they had gone out for lunch. The lobby had no shortage of derelicts and concerned citizens, voicing their complaints to whoever would listen.

Bay ignored them all as he walked up the counter, not bothering to stand in the short line.

A stocky lady, whose name was something along the lines of Lucy or Linda, stood behind the front desk. "Hello, Mr. Collins, do you have an appointment with anyone?"

"Is Detective Blake around?" He wasn't going to barge into his office this time. He'd see how much playing nice would get him.

The little brunette gave him an apologetic look. "He stepped out for lunch about twenty minutes ago."

Bay looked at the clock over her head. One fifteen; the lunch hour was almost over.

Darek having a late start for lunch meant he had probably talked to Lane and then left right after. Bay wondered how it had gone and decided to give him a call. Before he could take his phone from his pocket, he heard a voice behind him.

"Jesus, Bay, I told you I'd call you." Darek looked around and pulled Bay down the hall with him.

Bay met Darek's stare fiercely. "Look, I've been patient, but I'm going crazy sitting around the house, doing nothing. I need to know what's being done about Mia."

"We've put out an APB, notified missing persons, and we have an officer going around checking some of the hot spots. Places we've found some of the other victims."

Knowing that didn't comfort Bay in the least, mostly because he had been responsible for a couple of those body dumps himself. The killer was not likely to choose the same place for Mia. Missing persons was a joke. They would put out a few feelers and wait for something to happen on its own. Bay had worked with them before. He let out a breath of frustration as Darek continued.

"I'm going to interrogate him myself as soon as I get back from a meeting," he said.

"Fuck that," Bay said. "I'm tired of waiting. This isn't a case of Mia running away again. Max is using her to punish me. He fucked with her in the first place to fuck with me, just like he fucked Lizzy." Bay hoped to rile Darek up. He wanted him to act now instead of later.

Darek's eyes narrowed. "He didn't fuck her. He only wishes he did." He tugged at his tie, and Bay could tell that he had the man thinking about it.

"As far as you know," Bay said. "She might be too ashamed to tell you the truth. He could have used her, and you know what that kind of thing could do to a woman like Lizzy. It would make her feel so stupid she fell for it that she wouldn't want anyone, especially you, to know about it."

"I know what you're trying to do, Bay. And as much as I want to go in there and pound the guy's head until he talks, I'm not going to handle it that way."

"You don't have to. Just let *me* talk to him."

Darek put his hand on Bay's shoulder and leaned in closer. "Look, I'm handling this. I don't need you coming down here making it harder. You don't know what this has been like on my end of things. I've got the whole fucking department looking at me and watching my every goddamned move. They know that Max was my partner and my best friend, and some of them aren't on my side."

Bay smiled cruelly. "Damn, if that's the case, I guess they don't think too highly of you."

"All I'm saying is that Max has friends," Darek said. "He was a good cop, and he helped a lot of people around here. So, some folks are sitting around, wondering if he didn't do the world a favor. A vigilante cop taking out a cult? They're all looking at me and wondering if I'm fucking Lizzy or if I'm going to lose my shit. You aren't making it any better. And it's not going to help us find Mia any sooner."

Bay let out a growl of frustration. He looked over his shoulder and noticed they *did* have an audience. He pulled Darek into the first empty room. "Did you talk to Lane?"

"Yeah, I did. He pulled off the pedo ring story, and I think Lizzy bought it. I just hope she listens to me. I tried to convince her that saying anything to Max would be a bad idea."

"Yeah," Bay said. "I don't know if Lane told you, but he is Gough's son. I'm guessing this is a big revenge plot. He must have researched the case, found out who really did the crime, and did his homework. Although the others claimed they didn't say anything, there's no telling who they really talked to. If you've ever said anything—"

"I haven't," said Darek with a stern voice.

"I'm just saying, if you have, thinking it was harmless, it would be good to know."

"I haven't even told my therapist this shit," Darek spat the words and then turned to look over his shoulder.

"How's that going?" asked Bay. "Any more of your little episodes?" Darek's little problem had made it much easier for Bay to fuck with the detective. He was hoping to hear he'd had a hard time with it lately.

"The meds are doing their thing. I'm good." By Darek's stern tone, Bay knew he wasn't going to get anything out of him. "You just need to let me do my job."

Bay took a step back and raised his hands. "I'm staying out of the way. I just want a minute with him."

"You need to focus on someone else getting to him," Darek said. "That's what you should do. Put all of your angst over Mia into that task, and we'll be good."

"Is there any chance of him going to general population?" Bay knew it was a long shot, but he still had hope. Even a small window would suffice.

Darek shrugged. "You might be able to sway one of the guards to let him out into the courtyard when the others are there. Anything could happen to him, but I'm not guaranteeing that any of his fellow officers would throw him to the fucking wolves. It's a risky move too. You should be careful."

"I'm just looking for the right window," Bay said.

"How'd you do Logan?" asked Darek with a smug look. "Don't pretend that wasn't you."

"It was easy," Bay said. "No one knew him. I found a guard with marital and financial issues, and they owed me a few favors."

"Would the same guard take another chance?" Darek had a good point about using the same guard. The only problem with that was getting him back in the same place that Max was being held.

Bay shrugged. "I'm working on it. Do you have any dirt on anyone? Anyone owe you anything?"

Darek let out a long breath. "I'm not having this conversation with you here. Come on, man. I've got a meeting, and I promise as soon as I get back, I'm going down to see him."

"If you think of anything—"

"I'll let you know. Shit, Bay. I'm on your side. I promise."

"And I'm not going to rest until she's found," Bay said. "Stop acting so fucking surprised. If this was something going on with Raven or that fucking kid you're so concerned with, you'd tear the fucking world down. Why are you shocked when I have the same fucking reaction?"

Darek's shoulders slumped as he took a step back. "I'm sorry. I know this is tearing you up—"

"It's eating at me." He was only bothered because he was in a situation that he couldn't control. It was the worst possible scenario for him, and he was going to keep on until he got his moment alone with Max. "All I need is a minute with him. I just need to look him in the eye and..."

"And what?" Darek asked. "You have a child coming, Bay. You should step back and let us do our jobs. Focus on your family. Your wife. I'm sure she needs you right now."

Bay hadn't told Lila anything. He knew he needed to take care of that as soon as possible, but he had hoped he'd have answers for her when he did. The look on his face must have told Darek something because he let out a breath. "Jesus, Bay. You haven't told her?"

"It's only just been twenty-four hours. I was hoping that we'd have answers. That I'd have a body. Something."

"Maybe we'll find her alive. There's still hope."

Bay shook his head. "Nah, she's gone. I can feel it. Besides, whatever he's done to her, I'm pretty sure that she'd rather be dead than suffering. Or worse, living with the horror of it. My Mia is dead."

CHAPTER 5

LANE

After leaving the station, Lane drove out to Nona's house. The place looked strange with a cleaning truck out front. The police had called to tell him that they would be cleaning up the house once all the evidence was collected, and someone would have to sign off that everything was as clean as possible.

As he got out of his car, a man met him at the front door. "Excuse me, sir, are you family?"

"Yes," said Lane, not wanting an argument. "I'm here to sign off on the cleaning job."

"We had a detective stop in for a little more evidence, so we're just finishing up in the closet. We've taken the carpet up. It couldn't be cleaned, and most of it was already cut out in patches."

Lane tried not to think of the state the room had been in. The blood had stained the floor and seeped nearly into the bedroom. There was so much. "Thank you."

"No problem. Are you the victim's husband?"

"Fiancé," he said, knowing Nona had wanted it that way. In his heart of hearts, he knew it would have never worked out, but it didn't matter now.

"Sorry for your loss," the man said. "I'll just get finished up here, and I'll get that form to sign. It won't be but a few minutes."

"It's all good, thanks." Lane walked inside and went to Nona's desk to look for her address book. He was going to have to call her family and friends, including her aunt, who had already been informed of her death but had been waiting on Lane to give her more details. He wondered if he should get it over with. It wasn't like he could feel any worse.

He looked into her drawer and found her address book. He flipped through and wondered who was important enough to warrant a phone call. For the moment, he decided to just call her aunt Mary.

Before he dialed, he walked over to the couch and sat down. Like usual, he put his foot up on the coffee table. It was something he'd done a million times, and he'd thought nothing of it. But now, something caught his eye.

A tiny stain.

A little round drop of dried blood was on the sole of his shoe. His heart began to race, and his eyes burned. He remembered the day before and the blood that he'd stepped in. It must have splattered up onto his shoe.

He thought he'd gotten it all off. One of the officers had sent it back to him after collecting the evidence. He had thought they'd cleaned it up, but he couldn't help but wonder: had they left the one tiny spot to fuck with him?

With the cleaning crew still working at the other end of the house, he walked into the kitchen and stopped at the sink to take off his shoe. He turned on the hot water and let it run a minute while he scratched the blood off with his fingernail.

Everything that had happened came back to him. The blood sloshing under his foot, the slurpy sound of thick, wet carpet, and the way Nona's eyes looked up at him. She was lying there with her intestines a mangled mess in her lap and her face in a permanent scowl.

All he could think about was how he'd carried that part of her around with him. He put the shoe under the water and tried to scrub his sole clean. He had to get it clean.

He was just about to really lose it when he heard footsteps behind him. "So, yeah, we're finished up in the back. If you want to go check it out." The man's tone dropped a little when he walked into the room. "Are you okay?"

"Yeah, sorry. I had a damn spot on my shoe." He grabbed a rag from the counter and dried the shoe off before putting it back on his foot. "I'll just sign that when you're ready." He was sure his face showed all his emotions, but the man turned away, took a clipboard from one of the others, and passed it over.

Lane took the clipboard, and when he poised his pen, the other cleaner cleared his throat. "Sir, you really should go check out the room and make sure there's no problem with anything."

Lane shook his head. "I'm sure you guys did a bang-up job. Thank you very much." He scrawled his name and passed the clipboard back to the first man.

"It's cool, dude," said the first guy. He looked at his friend like he needed to let it go.

Once they had gone, Lane walked back over to the couch and kept his feet firmly planted on the floor. He didn't need anything else to mess with his head. "I have to get through this."

He dialed the number to Aunt Mary's house. She was probably the only person left on the planet who had a landline. She answered the phone with a weak voice, sounding more frail than usual. "Hello?"

"Aunt Mary, it's Lane. How are you holding up?"

"As good as I can," she said. "I always feared something like this would happen to her. She was too much of a free spirit and so flighty. I told her the last time we talked that she should settle down with you. Her clock was ticking, you know, and I knew how much you two really loved one another."

Lane felt like a knife was twisting in his gut. "Yeah, well, we talked about it actually. She didn't mention you two had discussed it."

"Well, I guess it's okay to tell you now, but she told me, she said, 'Aunt Mary, you just don't know how he makes me feel. I love him more than anything, but I don't know if I'm good enough for him or not.' She said she thought about moving south. It was all she talked about. I told her I'd support her decisions like always. I have my church and the ladies down at the bingo hall. If it weren't for them, I wouldn't be able to make it through, you know?" Her voice broke.

Lane hadn't told her the horrible details of Nona's death and didn't plan to. She knew that Nona had been murdered, and she had asked him not to tell her the worst of it. She had a bad heart, and she knew it wouldn't do her any good.

Lane had no idea that Nona and Mary had those conversations, and he didn't want to make Mary think that he didn't appreciate all her niece had been in his life. "I was calling to tell you that I just got her house released, so I'll be able to go through everything."

"I trust you to make the right decisions with all of that, Lane. I don't have room or the need for any of her things. If you could just take the majority and sell it, I would get more use out of the money." She cleared her throat and sniffled into the phone. "I would like a few of her personal things, things she loved, you know? If you could handle that for me, I'd appreciate it."

"I'll handle it," Lane said. "Don't worry about it. I'll ship you a few things. I haven't been able to talk to the funeral director, but when I do, I'll make arrangements for you to get her ashes."

"You're too good to me, Lane. You've always been so good to us both, and I want to thank you for that."

Lane didn't know what to feel about that. Nona had died because of him. If she hadn't been in his life, then she'd still be alive to talk to her Aunt and ask for life advice.

"It's nothing," he said. "She was a good girl. She deserves the best, you know? I'll make sure that I take care of her."

They talked for a few more minutes, and when Lane felt like she was finally going to be okay, he ended the call.

Sitting in the house alone, he kept expecting to look around and see her, but that was never going to happen. If it did, it would only be a figment of his imagination. He leaned forward and put his head between his knees. He needed to get it together. It had already been a long fucking day, and he was exhausted. He hadn't slept at all the night before. It wasn't possible with Nona's death mask staring him in the face every fucking time he closed his eyes.

The phone rang, and he sat up and answered. "Yeah, Darek?"

"Hey, I thought I'd call and check on you."

"I'm at Nona's getting shit straight," Lane said. "The guys just left from cleaning it up, so I hope you had all the evidence you needed because I'm going to sell most of her shit and donate the rest."

"Yeah," Darek said. "And having Max in custody, we're sure that there won't be a problem."

"Well, I hope so. I heard you came by. Well, I assume it was you. Did you swing over after the meeting for more evidence?"

Darek paused. "No, I haven't. It must have been someone else."

"The cleaners said a detective. I assumed you. They didn't specify if it was a man or a woman." Lane wondered who had been in the house, and he had an uneasy feeling.

"It might have been Lizzy," Darek said. "She's on this case like her ass is on fire. She's been in and out of the office, and it's a safe bet she wanted to make one more pass through the crime scene."

"Could you make sure?" Lane asked.

"Sure, but I wouldn't worry. It's common even for one of the other cops to check out the cleaners."

"Okay, just let me know," Lane said. "I think I'll try and stay the night here. I'm not sure that I can make it, but Bay has enough shit going on. He's not dealing with what's happening in a healthy way, and I can't fucking handle the stress. Since you have Max, there shouldn't be any reason to worry, right?"

"You're good. I can have an officer drive by if you want." Darek was a good friend to be concerned. "As for Bay, he doesn't handle anything emotional well. He doesn't really have the ability. He's already convinced that Mia is dead."

"What do you think?" Lane asked. "Do you think that asshole didn't kill her the first chance he got? I didn't want to tell Bay, but I think she's gone too."

"Bay's sure of it, but considering that Max had a relationship with

Mia, there's a chance that she's still alive. I'm going to do my best to get to the bottom of it. I'm going in to meet with him in five minutes. The guards are getting him ready now. Bay showed up earlier, throwing a fit to see him, but I told him to go home and handle his shit. He hasn't even told his wife anything yet."

"He's afraid for her health," Lane said. "She's carrying his child, and despite the fact that I know he loves Mia, there isn't anyone on the earth that he loves more than that child."

That was just how Bay worked. He loved himself more than anything, and he would naturally see his child as a part of himself.

"I know," Darek said. "I just wanted to make sure you're good and that you know I'm going to nail this guy's head to the fucking wall for you, man. Nona was a good girl. She deserved better."

"Thanks, man." Lane's chest swelled with anger, and he wished he could react the same way that Bay did, by lashing out at the world. Lane was furious, but he just couldn't let himself go there. He had to stay busy. There wasn't anything he could do for her now.

They ended their call, and he eased back in the chair. There was one more thing he could do. One that he *had* to do. He had the number dialed before he could think of what he would say.

"Hey, boss." Jennifer's voice matched her lively personality, and with everything around him dead and dying, he needed it.

In an instant, he changed his whole purpose for calling. He wasn't going to back out on her like he'd planned. "Hey, how's it going? Is business good?"

"Business is fabulous, but I hope that's not the only reason you called. Didn't you want to hear my voice?" She was so flirty, and he could see the smile on her face as he closed his eyes. It was the best image he'd imagined in the last few hours. Even though guilt was burning him up inside, he had to let it go. He had to live.

"Yeah, that's part of the reason, but the truth is, I might have to stay in New York a little longer. I've had another emergency come up." He wasn't going to explain what had happened. He was sick of explaining himself, and the last thing he wanted to do was relive all of the wretched moments from the past day.

"Oh no," she said, sounding sincere. "I'm so sorry. You just can't catch a break, can you?"

"I guess not," he said, feeling like a tool. "I'll need you to keep things afloat down there for at least a few more days. I guess at this point, I'll just call you when I'm on my way home."

"I can't wait to see you," she said. "There's so much I need to tell you. You're, like, so behind on the kitchen gossip." She gave a little giggle.

"I'm looking forward to hearing it," he said. "Maybe we'll have to get together outside of work, and you can catch me up." He shocked himself for making it more than it should be, but she was a nice girl, and he needed a good distraction.

"I'd love that," she said. "You could call me on my cell later if you need someone to talk to. I don't ever do anything but go home at the end of shift and watch old episodes of Jersey Shore."

He couldn't help but smile because Nona had loved that show too. "Maybe I will." He wasn't going to make any promises. But he sure felt better knowing that there was light at the end of his dark tunnel.

CHAPTER 6

DAREK

Waiting to talk to Max took longer than Darek expected, but that was only because the guards were taking their sweet time. He hoped that none of them were particularly close to his ex-partner. While he waited in the room, he kept his eyes peeled to see how they would react to the dirty cop.

The guards came in holding Max by each arm because his hands were cuffed in front of him. They gave Darek a nod. "Do you want him cuffed to the table?"

Max wore a shit-eating grin. Darek knew that having him cuffed to the table was probably the smart thing to do, but it was also going to make him look like a fool who was scared of a confrontation.

"We're good," said Darek. "We're old buddies, Max and I, so I'm sure he'll behave like a gentleman."

Laughter erupted from Max, whose mocking tone was unmistakable. "Yeah, we have a real bromance, man." He met Darek's eyes, shaking his cuffs. "I'd give you a high-five, but as you can see, I'm a little tied up here."

"I'll be right outside," said Officer Patrick, who turned and walked out the door.

Darek looked down at Max, who took his chair and did his best to move it closer to the table. "Where is Mia?"

"Aw, is that why you came to see me?" Max asked. "I had hoped it was because you found out who my old man is."

"Was," Darek corrected. "I found out who your old man *was*."

Max glared at Darek with narrowed eyes, angry at the detective's taunting. Darek watched Max struggle to regain his composure.

The smile slid back on his ex-partner's face. "And what did your girl think of that?"

Darek shrugged. "She doesn't know what to think of it. She had defended your father, you know? She told me that she thought he was innocent, and she was out to prove it." He had steered her away from it, and she was still angry with him over that. It turned out to be the right call.

Max nodded. "So now I just get to sit back and wait for this all to fall apart. It must be eating at you, wondering when I'm going to tell Lizzy everything. When she knows, it's going to tear you apart, and you know it."

"I'm more concerned about Mia. If you have her somewhere, don't make this shit any worse on yourself by letting her die. If she's already dead, have some fucking respect and tell me where to find her."

"Who am I showing respect to?" Max asked. "You? How about Bay Collins? You think that asshole deserves my respect? He's the one who organized everything."

"We're not going to waste time talking about Bay," Darek said. "You got your jab in. You fucked his girl, and you tried to fuck mine. Now let's stop with the petty shit. You're a coldhearted killer, remember? You're too badass for this weak-sauce bullshit."

Max laughed. "It's so much fun, though. Riling you up is so easy. You've always been a weak cop. I've seen you with Lizzy, and it's obvious that she wears the pants when it comes to the job and your partnership there. I just wondered if she took charge like that in the bedroom too."

Darek sighed. "Where's Mia? She's got family; a sister, a mother, people who love her. At least let's give them some closure if you've already killed her. It could go a long way in making you comfortable later."

The words seemed to amuse him. "I'm not worried about being here, bro."

"You should be."

Max shook his head. "No, because I'll end up accomplishing what I want. You'll see. I'll have the last laugh, my friend."

"Then what are you waiting for? Tell me all about it. How you devised a clever plan and carried it through. How you killed Alicia David once you no longer needed her."

"Alicia." Max closed his eyes and smiled as if he had fond memories of the girl. "She could suck cock like a champ. I can't tell you how many times I unloaded into that throat of hers, and she never missed a drop."

"I saw what you did to her," Darek said, leaning forward. "It's hard to believe you'd give that up. I guess you had all you needed from her? Did she know a lot about the Zodiacs?"

"She knew enough," Max said. "Alicia was good about doing what she was told. She trusted me wholeheartedly." His smile faltered a moment, and Darek couldn't help but wonder if Max missed his partner in crime.

"Where's Mia, Max? Come on and tell me."

"You know I can't do that," Max said.

Darek sighed. This was just the kind of attitude he didn't want from Max. As long as he didn't tell them where Mia was, he still maintained a little bit of control. He was still on a power trip and trying to hold on to it on the inside.

"You should be happy," he said. "I'm going to keep my mouth shut about you and your friends. For a while, at least. As long as I feel like I'm safe in here. If you try anything stupid, like put me in general population, or if your boy Bay thinks he's going to be able to pop me off like he did his buddy in here, then he's mistaken. You want to talk about a partner in crime? Bay's the one who should be sitting right here with me. Did you know he popped Hannah? Or Finn? Did you know that he did that?"

Darek's blood began to boil. He had long suspected what had happened with the others, but he never had solid proof until right then. But was Max telling the truth? Bay was certainly capable, and he'd all but admitted to having Logan killed.

"We're not here to talk about Bay," Darek said.

"Okay, let's talk about you, Darek. What is your part in all of this? You've covered up an entire investigation, and I have to say, I applaud you for managing to not only cover up your misdoings, but you also managed to nail your partner. Talk about the ultimate distraction. But then again, Lizzy is pretty easy like that. At least, I found her to be."

Darek's temper got the best of him, and he got up and leaned over in Max's face. "Where is she?"

He wished he would have just let Bay in to take care of Max. Darek wanted to punch him in his smug face so badly. He couldn't even deal.

Officer Patrick was right outside, and he walked over and stood closer to the door. Darek waved him off. He didn't need the man overhearing anything. He turned back to Max. "Look, I'm sorry about what happened to your old man, but Mia didn't have shit to do with that."

"No, she's just someone who Bay cares about," Max said. "I finally found the one person I could use to get to him, so why would I ruin that? You know, when he punched me after I fucked her, I knew then just how much he cared, and I knew I would use Mia to get my revenge. I mean, don't get me wrong. I had a great time with her. He's taught her well, and let me tell you. She's properly trained. I would have taken her for my pet if I was really serious about her."

Darek wanted to tell him how Mia didn't want him any more than Lizzy had, but Max's temper was just as bad as Darek's. If Darek riled him up too much or made him feel threatened, he was going to make sure they never found Mia.

"Give me a clue," Darek said, hating the pleading tone in his voice. "Anything. You texted me all those times, wanting to communicate. So let's talk now."

Max shook his head slowly. "It sucks to be so helpless, doesn't it? I imagine that's how my old man felt when he was locked up all those years. He'd had it rough enough already in life. Do you know he served our country? Not that it mattered in the end. He couldn't even get anyone to listen to him when he said he was innocent."

Darek was responsible for putting Gough in the position to be found with Emily Johnson. If Darek hadn't left Emily where he had, if he'd left her in the woods or even at the millhouse, no one would have blamed Gough. The man might still be alive.

But Darek had tried to do the right thing. Just like he was trying to do the right thing now by finding Mia. "So that's it? You're not going to give me anything?"

Max smiled. "Not a chance."

Darek walked out of the interrogation room. "Get him back to his cell."

He stormed down the hall and headed back to his desk. On the way, his phone buzzed in his pocket.

"Yeah?" he answered.

"It's me," said Bay. "Did you ever get to talk to the asshole?"

"I just did, but he's not talking. Which is good when it comes to us, but not Mia." He had hoped he'd have better news for Bay.

"Fuck him. He's going to use her as leverage, isn't he?"

"He likes the power, so yes." Darek tried to take a few calming breaths and ducked into the bathroom. "He thinks it's going to give him an advantage."

"Meet me at my house tonight. I have Lane coming too. We need to regroup."

Darek didn't think getting away from Lizzy would be a problem. She was still wanting to keep her distance since Reed was suspicious of them. Reed's problem with them having a relationship was dangerous to both of their careers.

"Yeah," Darek said. "I'll be able to make it. I'll see you there."

CHAPTER 7

BAY

B ay sat in his study, looking at Lila's portrait that hung over the fireplace. She had given it to him as a Christmas gift some years earlier. Although it was pretty risqué, he had hung it in the downstairs room so everyone who entered could see what a knockout he was with.

When Bay met Lila, she had it all—or so he assumed. She was not only the prettiest girl he'd ever seen at the time, but she came from money and was a favorite among the others in her sorority. Unfortunately, her level of common sense gave new meaning to dumb blonde, but while she wasn't the brightest bulb in the box, she had book smarts, which was good enough for Bay. The rest only made her more malleable, and that was something Bay could work with.

He looked into her painted eyes, which were nothing more than a couple of brush strokes carefully placed on the canvas, and he wondered what he would tell her about Mia. The shock was going to do a number on her, and there was no getting around that.

The doorbell rang, and while it played out the chiming tune, he looked up at the monitor hanging in the corner of his room. Lane was at the door. Darek walked up behind him, and the two shook hands.

Bay went to the door, and when he opened it, he found Darek

patting Lane on the back. The man was clearly upset about everything going on.

"Come on in," Bay said. "You're both right on time." He led them to the study, opting to keep things in the private room in case any of the staffers were lurking around. "Have a seat." He pointed to the small sitting area around the fireplace where Lila's half-naked body sprawled out on the canvas above them.

Lane's eyes went to the portrait as he sat, and a moment later, so did Darek's. The thing was unavoidably larger than life, and probably too big for the space, but that was just how he liked it. A little overwhelming. Just enough to make the other two men uncomfortable. He liked to throw people off balance. Through the years, it had made things more interesting to him when he was the only one who wasn't out of sorts.

He cleared his throat and grabbed the two men's attention. Darek was the only one brave enough to mention it. He put his arm over the back of the couch and gave the painting a sideward look. "Is that your wife?" he asked in a tone that clearly showed his surprise.

Bay walked over to the bar to pour them all a drink. "Yes. Isn't she phenomenal? Can you imagine how amazing our child will be?" Their baby would no doubt have the blondest hair and the palest eyes.

Darek didn't take his eyes off her. "She's beautiful."

"The likeness is striking," said Lane. "Who was the talented artist?"

Bay smiled. He walked the two drinks over and handed them off. "I'm not sure, but they sure got an eyeful, didn't they?"

"I'd say no more than we have," said Darek. "Lizzy would never pose like that."

"Nona would have," Lane said with a sad smile. "I have a few photographs I'll cherish."

Bay grabbed his own drink and walked over to stand near the mantle. "Speaking of your dearest Nona, I can't help but mention Darek's visit to Maxwell Gough behind bars."

Darek nodded. "He isn't going to talk, so we're good for now, but I can't guarantee for how long. He is angling for his safety, which I can't blame him for. He knows we want to take him out, and I know he's enjoying dangling Mia over our heads. He hates you, Bay. Like, a lot."

Bay couldn't give a fuck if the asshole liked him. "Well, the feeling is mutual," he said. "So, fuck him."

"Well, he said that when you punched him, you showed him how much you really cared about Mia. That was what he wanted to use her for. To figure out what you loved most. I'd say you're very lucky to have hidden your unborn child away."

"I'm going to have to ask her to come back into town," Bay said. "I'm not entirely sure how to tell her Mia is missing and presumed dead via the telephone."

Darek shook his head. "No, you're right, and she's good now. It should be safe. We have the killer locked up. Now our focus needs to be finding Mia while there is still hope that she's alive. Part of me thinks that if she were dead, perhaps he would have already fessed up. But I'm not a hundred percent on that. Max has shown me a whole different side to himself, so I have to assume that everything I know is the opposite of what it is."

"Well, I'm not going to sit around with false hope, which is why I want to find Mia before I tell her family," Bay said. "Lila will need answers. I want to make sure I have some kind of closure for her."

"I'm not sure I can help," Darek said. "I need to focus on what Lizzy and I have cooking. If I'm going to keep walking this thin line, I need to make sure that my focus stays where it is."

Lane spoke up. "What if we go and find his brother? Otis Gough, Jr. might just know what his brother is up to, and if he doesn't, then maybe he'll have some clue as to where he's keeping Mia."

"That's a good plan," said Bay. "There's also a chance that his brother doesn't know shit, but that's a chance I'm willing to take." Bay looked at Darek. "Did he say anything that might tip you off to where she could be?"

"No," Darek said. "He's not going to give us anything, but the brother is a good idea. Just don't go and piss him off. I wouldn't tell him who you are or what your intentions are."

"Don't worry," said Bay. "I'm going to tell him my name is Detective Blake." He smirked, but Darek didn't seem to find him funny.

"You can think of something better, I'm sure," Lane said. "I think we're going to be surprised when we find him. We'll know right away if he knows us, and if he doesn't seem to, the aliases should work just fine."

"Call me if you think he's in on it," Darek said. "He could have Mia, and he could be in on this with his brother for all we know. A case like this, it's not unthinkable for him to have had help. Especially since he's so close to the department. Let's just hope if we find them, they have Mia, alive and well."

"Still not holding my breath," said Bay. He didn't want to be disappointed when they found her in pieces. He had a feeling that Max had ripped her apart like he had Nona. "Did you find the phone he used to text us with?"

"No," said Darek. "It was never recovered. Which leads me to think that he's got it stashed someplace he's used to frequenting. I've searched his car and his desk personally."

Lane didn't look convinced. "He could have just tossed the fucking phone in the river."

"He probably did the same with Mia." Bay hated to be morbid, but it was like Max to leave his victims down at the river. "Maybe we should try looking there. We should go down to the storage containers too. See if he's got her locked up in there."

"Be my guest," Darek said. "I've already looked. But I didn't have much to go on. I'd start with the brother."

Lane nodded. "Has Max already called his family and warned them that he's been arrested?"

Bay nodded at the question, which he was curious to hear the answer to. If Max had an accomplice, he might have already warned them.

"No," Darek said. "He hasn't called anyone, and he's not talking to the press. Neither are Lizzy and I for now. There might come a time we have no choice, but she's in agreement."

"Did you get anything on the murder weapon yet?" asked Bay. They had recovered a huge knife from the scene.

"Not yet."

"Fuck, man," Bay said. "Do you cops have anything at all? What's the fucking holdup? That should have been the first fucking thing they looked at. Give it to Cobb. He can compare the fucking wounds."

"The team is on it," Darek said coolly. "I can't rush them, or it will look suspicious. I'm not going to make any waves. Even the slightest hint of misconduct, and I'll be thrown off the case." Darek had made enough waves by arresting Max, and even though Bay knew it, he wanted shit to move as fast as possible.

"Look," said Darek, who leaned forward in his chair. "I think you'd do best to just focus on figuring out how you're going to kill him. Leave the detecting to me."

"And me," said Lane. "I'm going to keep on the trail of Max's past. I told Kenneth Warner to get back in touch if he remembered or found anything else."

"Maybe the brother will tell you something you didn't know," Darek said. "I'd ask him about the case and anything he knows about why his brother might decide to go vigilante and turn serial killer."

"We'll ask everything we can," Lane said firmly. "First, we have to find him. I'll get on that tonight."

"You can stay here, and I'll help," Bay said.

"Yeah, you shouldn't be alone, and that will give you some focus," said Darek. "I'm going to go home and talk to my partner. I need to figure out what our next move is. She's in the process of collecting every ounce of evidence for the case against Max. She wanted to make sure that every tee is crossed. We're already not the class favorites, and this hasn't helped. Even those who know Max is guilty still don't trust a cop that would turn on another, and in this case, that's me."

"That's ridiculous," said Lane. "You were just doing your job."

"For once," Darek said. "I probably could have solved this case six times over if I was really trying. I have never had such a hard time, and Lizzy makes it all a challenge."

"I bet," said Bay. "And have you heard anything from Raven lately?"

"No, she and I are through. I'm with Lizzy, and I don't talk to her unless there is something I can do for Noah."

"Yeah, make it about the kid. I bet Lizzy is not buying that excuse." Bay liked to rib Darek, and he smiled as Darek shifted uncomfortably in his seat.

"Fuck that," the detective said. "I'm not using the kid. He's been through enough. Besides, if I wanted her, I'm pretty sure I could have her."

Bay laughed. "You're right. I'm pretty sure if me or Lane wanted her, the same would be true."

Darek moved to the edge of his seat. "Fuck you. Focus on Max's brother and keep the fuck out of my love life."

"Raven's lucky, isn't she?" asked Lane to Darek. "That really could have been *her* instead of her cousin."

Darek got to his feet. "Yeah, she's lucky. I wish her the best. But Lizzy is my future. I'm going to make the most of it once this is all over." With that, he downed the last of his drink. "I need to be going. Good luck on your hunt."

Bay walked him out and then met Lane, who had followed as far as the living room. "So, where do we start?"

Lane stared down at his phone. "I've already got his address. I say we get some sleep and go first thing in the morning."

"Good job," said Bay. "Count me in."

CHAPTER 8

DAREK

With the case heating up and Lizzy demanding that they take some time away from one another, Darek didn't expect to see her until he got down to the station. So when he heard his doorbell ring early on Sunday morning, he reluctantly rolled out of bed and dragged ass to the door, surprised to find Lizzy standing there.

Darek rubbed his eyes. "Am I dreaming?"

Lizzy smiled and stepped inside.

"To what do I owe a visit at this hour?" he asked. As soon as he shut the door, he turned and pulled her into his arms. "Miss me?"

"I woke up early this morning and couldn't go back to sleep, and yes, I missed you." She rolled her eyes like it was the last thing she wanted to admit, and he kissed her hard on the mouth to show her how grateful he was that she'd shown up.

She pulled away and looked him in the eyes. "Darek. I didn't come here for a hookup. I thought if I could get you up—"

"Oh, you got me up all right." He smirked, but she released a sigh.

"As I was saying, I didn't come by for a hookup. I wanted to talk about the case."

It had been too many days since they were intimate, and all she wanted to do was talk. Darek wasn't having it. "Let's go talk between the sheets. It's Sunday morning, the murder weapon is still being tested, and there isn't a soul in the department, including Reed who would expect you to be working right now."

"He also wouldn't expect me to be in your bed." She gave him a scolding look. "Come on, let's talk about what happened. I'm a bit worried about you. I mean, Max is our killer, and you're not dealing with it in a healthy way."

"I guess I'm just resilient, or maybe numb." He shrugged and lifted her off her feet. "You can talk all you want, but you're doing it from the bedroom."

She giggled as he carried her to his bed, and when he tossed her on it, she kicked off her shoes as he settled back under his covers. "Fine," she said, crawling up beside him where he held the covers back for her.

He wrapped his arms around her and closed his eyes. "*This* is what I've been missing. Having you in my bed every morning. I still think you should move in. We could keep your apartment as a decoy, and no one in the department would have to know."

"I think the bureau checks up on its agents from time to time, but I appreciate you missing me so much." She brushed his hair back from his forehead. "It makes a girl feel wanted."

"I wish this was all over. I'm tired of this fucking nightmare and everything that comes with it. I want to wake up next to you and live my life with you, Lizzy. Don't you want the same thing?"

They had talked casually about marriage before, and he knew that she had no intentions of having a family, but he hoped that he could change her mind on that one. Especially since he'd met Noah. Seeing the little one, being able to help him, it really had opened his heart to the idea of having a child of his own.

"I *do* want you in my life, Darek. I just don't know what that means. It's not like we live normal lives."

She had a point, but Darek couldn't see his future with anyone else. No one else would understand his line of work, how it affects a marriage. No one else would know the struggle like Lizzy. That was what he needed, right?

"But you don't want to do this forever, do you?" Darek asked. "I mean, don't you want to raise a family?"

"If you think I'm the kind of woman who would give up her career to stay home and be a mother, you're mistaken, Darek. That's not me. It's not who I am."

"It's not a bad way to be, but you could have a child and still work. I'm not a Neanderthal who thinks you'd have to give up anything to raise a kid. I'd help all I could, but wouldn't that be amazing? A little you and me running around."

Lizzy closed her eyes, and Darek felt the vibration of her laughter seconds before he heard it. "Just what the world needs," she said under her breath. Darek didn't know whether to take offense or not. "Look, that's just not in my cards. I mean, maybe someday, but not now, not—"

"With me?" he asked.

"I didn't say that," she said. "I think you'd make a wonderful father to someone if given the chance, but I have things I want to do, and I don't plan on taking nine months off, plus hindering myself for another twelve years until the kid doesn't need a babysitter. Sorry, it's not for me."

Darek felt a part of his spirit dim, but he thought Lizzy was worth it enough to sacrifice certain things. "Then you'll just have to be my baby," he said, pressing his cock into her thigh. "You gonna let me baby you? Spoil you?"

"Maybe a little." She put her leg up over his hip and then ran her hand down to his waist. "But I still just want to talk about the case. You haven't told me how the talk went with Max yesterday. Did he give you anything?"

Darek shook his head. "Nothing. He's being stubborn, but I say we let him stew a bit."

"I want to reach out to his family and see what triggered all of this vigilante killer stuff," Lizzy said. "He must have been trying to seek revenge on the other victims."

Darek frowned. "Other victims?"

Lizzy nodded. "I have a theory. If his father was fucking around

45

with other little boys, then he must have been messing around with his own kids."

"I don't know, Lizzy. Some pedophiles don't mess with their own kids, you know? They see it as wrong, whereas they don't see other people's children as taboo."

"But maybe he *was* mistreating his own children, and maybe Max had developed an unhealthy attachment. I mean, this is all just theory, but let's assume this man was guilty of molesting every boy he knew. Then why kill a girl? What if he still was innocent of the crime?"

Darek shook his head. "Come on, Lizzy. Who knows what that sick fuck was thinking? And his son is locked up for multiple murders. Do you really think the father of a criminal like Max was incapable of killing? That Max didn't learn the behavior somewhere?"

"All I'm saying is that we need proof, Darek. You know that's what we do, right?"

Her sarcasm was not unnoticed, and he held her tighter and brought his lips to hers. "Let's stop talking before we end up fighting. Besides, *this* is really what we do, isn't it?" He rolled his hips, grinding against her. She had her leg raised over his, which made it easy to press against her, and she closed her eyes as if pleasure rolled through her.

"You're not being fair," she said. "And it's not that I want to fight."

"Then don't." Darek pulled her across him, and she ground her hips against him, giving him a lip lock that left him breathless. He tugged the hem of her blouse, and she sat up to strip it off, showing him her black lace bra. It wasn't a color she wore that often, but he liked the contrast on her milky skin. It reminded him of Raven, but he pushed the thought of the other woman aside and focused on Lizzy. Everything he wanted was in his arms, and he would never have to look any further than her.

She reached and pushed down his briefs, exposing his erection. He cupped her breasts and rolled his thumbs over her tight nipples. Then he rose up and took them one at a time with his lips, sucking and teasing. "God, I've missed you, baby."

"I've missed you too." After pushing up her skirt and moving her panties to the side, Darek slowly moved his way inside her.

She rode him with slow and deliberate strokes, and he looked up at her, watching how fucking amazing she could work him. He put his arm around her waist, and then in a quick motion, he was on top, settling himself deeper as her legs wrapped around his ass. As she moaned out, his pride swelled. "Fuck yeah."

It had been too long for the two of them, and Darek made the most of every touch, every kiss, and every ounce of pleasure he gave and received. Finally, after giving her a toe-curling orgasm, he found his own pleasure and was surprised when Lizzy didn't have him pull out.

"I love you," he said.

She searched his eyes for a moment, like it was much harder for her to say. But when she did, it made it all the more meaningful. "I love you too."

Darek kissed her as they lay together, still joined. "I wish this was all we had to do forever."

"Me too," she said. "But I love my job too much." She gave a little laugh. "Don't you?"

"Some days, yes. But others? Hell no. Compared to this? Fuck no. I'd take me and you like this over anything." He rolled over and laid against the cool mattress.

Before he could snuggle, she got up, found her top, and straightened her skirt. "We should go down to the lab and see if they have the weapon ready."

Darek groaned. "Are you serious? It's Sunday, baby."

"I told them not to rest until they had matched it to all of the victims. They had a lot to test, but Miles assured me that they would keep on it through the night."

Darek narrowed his eyes. "How did you manage that?"

"He didn't want the assholes who work Monday through Friday to get all the credit, so he worked from start to finish. He's sick of people taking credit for his work. He should be getting close."

"So, there was some blood evidence on the knife?" Darek asked.

"Initially, yes, they found blood. They just have to match it with a victim now."

"So, that would mean that so far, he probably hasn't. Or we would have heard something, right?"

"Not necessarily. Miles is probably waiting for the big reveal. He's a bit overdramatic." She rolled her eyes as if she didn't think too much of him.

"Let's get some breakfast first. You've made me work up an appetite." He sat up and moved to the edge of the bed. "I'm going to shower first, though. Want to scrub my back?"

"You go ahead. I'll make a few calls."

"You're killing me, Lizzy." He got to his feet and reluctantly went to his solo shower. As he set the water and undressed, he wondered if she wanted to try and talk to Max's family, knowing that Bay and Lane were going to head over first thing. A late-night text had revealed that they already knew where Otis Jr. lived. Darek would have to drag his feet and make sure he took charge of their day, starting with a nice, big breakfast.

CHAPTER 9

BAY

Cruising upstate with Lane to talk to Max's brother wasn't Bay's idea of a good time. But after waking up alone with still no word about Mia, he hoped the trip would at least get them closer to finding her.

"Do you want another one?" asked Lane, who pulled a spicy donut from the box that Bay had placed between them.

"No thanks. One of those is too many in one sitting." He didn't like eating junk food but had decided to see what the fuss was all about when the place first opened. Against his better sense, he'd developed a taste for them. "They're good but terribly bad for you."

Lane shrugged. "I worked out this morning. Plus, I'm starved."

Bay remembered when Lane was nothing but a chubby kid who got picked on every day of his life. Lane had grown up to be buff, but Bay couldn't help but think the man was going to regret the third donut later on in life. "You've already blown that workout with your second one."

"Why don't *you* work out?" Lane asked. "You have that amazing gym downstairs. Where were you this morning?"

"I work out at night," said Bay. "I like to have the place to myself, and besides, Mia and Lila are usually in there in the mornings." At least, Lila used to be. He'd made her stop her early morning workouts since the pregnancy, and now, all he allowed her to do was some stretching and walking.

"Well, I'm jealous. I hope you don't mind me making myself at home."

"Not a problem," Bay said. "I'm glad someone is getting some use out of it. Lila insisted we have it. I have to give her credit. I enjoy it more than going to the public gyms." He looked over as Lane took another donut out of the box and took a bite. "Feel free to use it again later. At this rate, I'm going to have to roll you out of the fucking car when we get back."

He picked the box up and moved it to the backseat of the rental.

"Hey, there are still more in there," Lane said.

"Which is why I didn't toss it out the window," said Bay with a monotone voice. "I can't believe a chef such as yourself, who prides yourself on fine Cajun cuisine, would be so tempted by something so basic and innutritious."

"Actually, I'm trying to figure out the recipe for a spicy beignet. I need something like this on my menu. Something that will set me apart."

"It would do that, all right." Bay didn't hate the idea, but he hoped Lane would do it with a bit more class.

Lane sighed. "I guess it's going to be a long fucking ride with you. I should be back at Nona's, getting shit ready to ship off, but instead, I get to play ride-along road trip with the Slayer."

Bay looked out the window and saw the landscape changing as they headed north. They had already been in the car on the open road for a little over a half hour. "How much longer to Otis Jr.'s house?"

"We have about twenty minutes, so not too long."

"Good," Bay said, taking out his phone to look at Mia's photo. "I've had my fill of road trips." The last one, he'd had to come home from alone.

"I don't mind it so much," said Lane. "But I'm ready to be on that plane home."

"You've got a lot waiting for you?" Bay asked, wondering how his social life was back home.

Lane shrugged. "I'm still talking to Jennifer. She's sweet, and I gave her a call last night. Her voice was enough to get me excited, you know? I felt kind of bad, all things considered, but—"

"Nona's dead," Bay said flatly. "You still need a means of release. I understand." Bay was getting about overdue for one himself, and he would need more than the soft lips of his servant, Jasmine, who was always eager to please. "I have to go to the club soon, or else I'll end up fucking the help again."

Lane grinned. "You bone your staff?"

"You saw Jasmine, didn't you? She's a goddess. I hired her because she's Rose Marie's niece, but she's useless without her aunt around. I put her to good use, on her knees of course. I was raised not to fuck the staff, but a blowjob doesn't count, right? Besides, she's giddy for me."

"Geez, I need your life." Lane slowed the car and turned off the main road, into a neighborhood where all the houses were too close together. The yards were so messy, one spilled over into the other.

"Which one of these shitholes does his brother live in?" asked Bay.

"That one on the end," said Lane. He pointed ahead to a brown house where a man stood out front, working on a motorcycle. "That's him."

Bay noted the man's facial features when he rose up and looked at the car as if he were policing the neighborhood.

"I can see the family resemblance," said Bay.

"He's a mean-looking motherfucker." Lane wasn't kidding. The man was ripped, and his long dark hair and neck tattoos made him look like the criminal in the family.

Bay wondered what the chances were that the man didn't know anything. Lane killed the car, and Bay got out. Otis was already walking over.

Bay stuck out his hand. "I'm Bay Collins." *Fuck an alias.* He wanted this asshole to know exactly who he was speaking to. "Are you Otis Gough, Jr.?"

The man hesitated to take Bay's hand. "Yeah, that's me." Despite the man's threatening appearance, he had a softer look in his eyes. "Look, I've already told your associates, I'm not interested in making a movie about my father. I'm not looking to cash in on a family tragedy. I've put all that behind me."

Lane and Bay exchanged a look, and Lane stepped forward to shake his hand too. "We're not with a production company."

"Or the press," said Bay.

Otis narrowed his eyes at them. "Then who are you with? Because no one ever comes here unless they want something."

"We just want to talk," said Bay. "Off the record. We're not here to exploit you in any way. I just need to ask you about your brother Max."

The man's chest swelled as he took a deep breath. "Shit, is he dead?"

Bay shook his head. "No, he's not dead."

Otis breathed a sigh of relief. "Good for him. I'm glad he's okay, but I'm afraid I'm not interested in anything he's gotten himself into." He took a step back and picked up his wrench.

Lane walked over to him. "That's a sweet bike."

"Thanks," he said, looking over his shoulder. "So, what has he gotten himself into now? Because I know you really don't give fuck all about my bike."

"Your brother is in jail," said Lane. "He's been arrested for committing several murders."

The man's face paled. "What? Murder?" He shook his head and closed his eyes. "I knew he'd end up in prison or dead over this bullshit. He never could let shit lie."

"Let what lie?" Lane asked.

Otis rolled his eyes. "Come on. You know who my father is, so don't pretend. My brother has been fucked up ever since our dad was falsely imprisoned for a crime he didn't commit. I tried to help Max out years ago, but that came back to bite me in the ass. He's got his own strange habits, and my wife didn't like him around the kids with his women, so I kicked him out. Then he got it in his head to be a cop.

I don't have a whole lot of respect for cops, but even I know my brother wasn't cop material. He was too sadistic. Too angry." He tossed the wrench to the ground with his other tools. "I'm not helping him out if that's why you're here."

Bay approached Otis and looked him in the eye. "No one expects you to do anything for your brother. In fact, I'm not sure you could help him even if you wanted to. But you might be able to help *us*. One of Max's victims is still missing. A young girl. My girl. Do you have any idea where he might take someone?" Otis was already shaking his head. "Do you know anything that could give us a clue?"

"Look, I'm sorry for your girl," Otis said. "I really am. But I kicked Max out because he was into some weird shit. The last straw was when I came home and found him with some wild, black-haired, emo chick tied up in the basement. That was too much for my wife. She told him he had to leave, and he packed up his things and hers, and they were both out of here."

"A black-haired girl?" Lane looked at Bay. "Was the first victim black-haired?"

"No, she was a blonde. But her name was Black Betty." Bay searched the man's eyes. "Does that name ring a bell?"

"No, I never asked her name," Otis said. "I just wanted him to get the fuck out before my kid saw what I saw. I don't know how he turned what happened to our father into his pass to do the things he does, but I know that girl. She was into it. I mean, the girls he was with were all consenting as far as I could tell."

Bay was the last person to judge Max for strange sexual proclivities, but the dark-haired girl was very interesting. "You say it was black hair? Was it dyed? Dark brown?"

"Black, like almost fucking blue. She was hot, but shit. The things she liked were fucking scary, you know?"

Bay's back stiffened. He knew one woman with black hair like that, and she just so happened to like a lot of kink in her life. She had also spent more than enough time with the Zodiacs, including him at his own fucking club.

Otis shrugged. "Not long after that, he joined the force. The two of them got a shitty apartment uptown, but I was done. My wife said if I ever tried to do anything for him again, she'd leave me. In case you can't tell, she's kind of all I have going for me."

Bay wasn't going to insult the man, but he wished he had more to tell him. "Was there any family property in the city? Did you ever hear him talk about a secret place or a place he liked to go?"

Lane spoke up. "Anything you could tell us would help."

"Sorry," said Otis. "I wish I could help. I probably already said too much. I'm not getting my family dragged into this. I remember how horrible it was with my father."

Bay looked into his eyes. He thought of the old man who had done time for his crimes, and how the man would probably hate him if he knew who he really was. Suddenly, there was a noise from the house.

"What's going on?" asked a skinny woman in a dingy gray shirt. She looked like her hair hadn't been combed in weeks, or washed.

"It's nothing, honey," Otis called back sweetly. "It's about Max. I told these gentlemen we don't want anything to do with it."

"You have a phone call," she said, standing in the doorway with no smile for Bay or Lane.

"I really should go," Otis said. "Thanks for coming by and telling me about Max, but he's not my problem anymore." He turned to walk away, and as he went into the house, Lane put his card in the man's toolbox and shut the lid, hoping he'd find it later. Bay thought it was pointless. The man was done talking.

"You ready to go?" asked Bay.

"Yeah," said Lane. "So much for getting those answers."

Bay didn't think they'd done that bad, but he kept the thought to himself.

CHAPTER 10

DAREK

Lizzy's voice was a welcome sound in the morning, but not when she was so adamant that they get to work. "Get up, Darek. I'm not going to be late today."

Darek rolled over with sleepy eyes and reached for her.

She slapped his hand away. "No! I'm not falling for it again. By the time we had sex and then went to breakfast, you made me miss my chance to check on the weapons yesterday. I'm not losing focus."

"We don't have to be the first people at the station, Lizzy. Let's snuggle a bit, and then we'll go in." He'd told her the night before that he wanted her in his bed in the morning, but he didn't mean for her to be there to kick him out. He meant morning sex.

"I mean it, Darek. Come on."

"We shouldn't go in together anyway. Reed will be on our ass if he sees us roll in at the same time. So, I'll just stay here while you head in first. I'll be right behind you."

"I can't believe you're being so lazy," said Lizzy. "After yesterday? You kept me in bed all day, and we didn't get anything accomplished."

Darek smiled. "Oh, I beg to differ. I accomplished a lot and so did you." He hadn't gotten off so many times in twenty-four hours since he'd been with Raven, but never with Lizzy. She was much more reserved.

"Stop it," she said. "You're going to make me blush, Detective." She reached for his hand. "Come on. You're getting up."

"Yes, I am, but not how you think." He couldn't help but laugh when she gave up and crossed her arms.

"I'm not laughing." Her tone was serious, and Darek could tell that he'd taken the playtime too far.

"Fine." He moved to the edge of the bed, and when he got to his feet, she handed him his pants and shirt. "But if I'm not sleeping in, you're driving me to work."

After he dressed, they headed down to the station, and on the way, Lizzy's mood hadn't improved. "I hope they have good news," she said as she drove into the parking lot.

"Me too," Darek said. "Then maybe you'll be in a better mood." He actually liked that she was serious about her job. It took a lot of drive and passion to stay so focused, and that was why he was so attracted to her. But he still liked to tease her.

"Darek, you know how much this means to me. This could be what seals the deal, and then we're done."

"And then what?" he asked.

She shrugged. "We see it through trial and move on to other things?"

He understood why she was sick of working on this case, but he had enjoyed working with her. With the case closing soon, they wouldn't have the chance to spend as much time together. Then again, they might be able to go public with their relationship, which would be even better.

They walked into the building and made their way down to the lab, where Miles stood with his superior who had a disappointed look on his face.

"I don't like that look," Lizzy said to the two lab techs. "Please tell me that you got it done."

"Oh, it's done, all right," said the other man. "I'm Joel. I ran the samples for Miles, and we have come to a conclusion."

Lizzy planted her hands on her hips. "Well, let's have it." She stared at the men like she could slap the two of them.

Joel took a deep breath as if trying to muster up the courage to speak. "I know this means a lot to you, but the only match we found was to Max. This weapon, to the best of my knowledge, was never used in any type of murder."

Her shoulders slumped. "Are you fucking kidding me?"

"I wish we were," said Miles. "I went through hours of testing, and nothing was matching up. I forgot to do Max's for a control first."

Darek's heart sank. How the hell was that possible? The victims had all been slaughtered with a knife that had a blade matching the weapon they'd found. "He won't walk, will he?"

Lizzy scowled. "Not if I can help it. We already had other evidence, including the positive ID from Noah and the fact that he hasn't denied anything."

Joel gave Lizzy an apologetic look. "You might want to get back to the scene of the crime or even his house. See if there is anything else you can bring in for us. Once we get back to our regularly scheduled fun, it could be a week or more before we have time for special requests."

"Fuck it," said Darek. "Let's go to his house. He might have more to find."

"The officers already went through the house with a fine-toothed comb." Lizzy let out a growl of frustration. "Come on." She didn't bother to thank the guys as she turned and stormed off.

Darek stayed back. "Hey, thanks. Even though the results sucked, I know you tried." Joel gave Miles a dirty look, and Darek hurried out after Lizzy, who was already halfway to the car.

"Can you believe that shit?" Lizzy asked. "He wasted all that fucking time for something he could have told me two days ago!"

"He fucked up. He's new, and he's trying to impress you."

"If he wanted to impress me, he could have gotten shit right the first time. So, I guess we're headed to Max's fucking house?"

"Unless," said Darek, who had an idea. "Why don't we go and talk to Marvin? He was close with Mia. He might have some more information that would help us out."

"That could be good, I guess. He is bound to know something, and now that he's got a clear head, who knows?"

Darek held out his hand. "I'll drive. You're too pissed off. I don't want to give you a loaded gun like the Rover. You'll be making ten-point hits on pedestrians." He hoped to make her laugh, but instead, she didn't even look at him as she passed him the keys and got in the passenger seat.

He climbed behind the wheel and found she wasn't any better. "Can you believe that shit?" she asked. "I mean, really?"

He had to hear about it the entire way to the hospital. He was glad when they finally parked, and Lizzy refocused her thoughts on Marvin.

They found his room and knocked on the door. "Marvin?" called Darek after there was no answer.

The girl with purple hair opened the door. "Oh, it's you. Marvin's waiting on his lunch. He's got his headphone on." She stepped away from the door and went to the chair to grab her jacket. "Hey, boo, I'm going out for a smoke. Do you want anything?"

Marvin shook his head and gave Darek a hard look. "Did you find her?"

"No, not yet," said Lizzy. She walked over by his bed, while Darek took the chair. "We had hoped that maybe we could ask you some more questions."

Darek could already tell that Marvin's demeanor had changed. He raked his IV hand through his hair and looked toward the window. "I don't have anything to help you."

"Maybe you do, though." Lizzy wasn't going to leave without questioning him, and Darek made himself comfortable, knowing it. "Did Mia ever talk about Max bringing her anywhere?"

Marvin shrugged. "She told me a few places they'd been together. That son of a bitch was a kinky man, and she was just as bad to go along with him."

"What do you mean?" Lizzy asked. "Where did he take her that was so bad?"

"They did it in the bathroom at the park, for one," Marvin said. "I told her she had better watch out, doing risky shit like that, but she laughed it off. She also said that they did it in his car in the police station parking lot. She only had a short time for lunch, herself."

Lizzy cleared her throat. "Did she ever say anything about a storage building, a container? Any type of place like that ring a bell?"

"She said that they went to a sleazy motel, and sometimes, he would blindfold her. She didn't seem to think it was a big deal. She trusted him because he was a cop, you know? So, he could have taken her anywhere, done anything, and I think she'd have been good with it."

"But nothing ever more specific?" asked Darek. Marvin looked like he was hesitating. "If there is anything you're holding back, please don't. Mia's life is in danger, if she's alive at all. But we have to act fast."

Marvin plucked at a stray thread on the blanket over his lap. "She's going to be pissed off at me for telling you this, but she said that he would blindfold her at the hotel and then he'd take her elsewhere. He liked to pretend to kidnap her. It was a type of roleplay for them. But she said it got to be too weird, so she told him she couldn't see him anymore. He lost it. They had a fight. She bailed."

Darek wanted to punch the man. "Why the fuck didn't you tell me this earlier? We had a whole conversation, and you never mentioned that."

"I knew that this time, it was for real," Marvin said. "I thought if I told you that this was their weird roleplaying thing, you'd stop looking for her. I want to keep that asshole behind bars. He stabbed me, okay? And I don't want anything to do with any of this shit anymore."

"Mia wouldn't let him leave you for dead," Darek said.

"No, but she's not in control. He is. He always was. That sick fuck, Bay, got her into that lifestyle, and she doesn't know anything but how to go along with it. She went back to him as if it was the lesser of two evils, but evil all the same. I don't want to be involved anymore. Could you please go now?"

Darek was stunned. "Are you fucking kidding me? Mia's your friend."

He shook his head. "She was. And I'm afraid she's gone now. So if whoever stabbed me ever gets out, he could come after me again. I'm unfinished business."

Lizzy sighed. "Don't give yourself too much credit, Marvin." She looked over the bed at Darek and gestured for him to wait outside.

He went to the hallway to find the violet-haired friend standing outside. "Are you done? Haven't you guys questioned him enough?"

"No, apparently we haven't," Darek said. "But since you're free, how about you tell me what made him change his tune? Did someone else come talk to him?"

The girl shook her head. "He just doesn't want to be blamed for what happened to Mia. He said he doesn't want to be involved."

"I can respect that," he said. "Did he ever tell you anything about his friend, Mia?"

She huffed. "That girl wasn't ever his friend. I'm the one who had to explain that to him. She was just using him for his talent, and she got him into a bunch of trouble. His true friends are the ones who are glad he's alive. We've taken turns up here to sit with him. He's afraid the man who stabbed him is going to walk, and he doesn't want to be alone."

Darek frowned. "The man who did this? He's all locked up. And he's never getting out."

With that, Lizzy appeared in the doorway behind him. "That was a lost cause," she said. "My record for the day is in the gutter."

The other girl rolled her eyes and went back into the room.

"How about we get something to eat and then pick this hunt up afterward?" Darek asked. Lizzy looked like she needed a break, and he could use a bite. She had dragged him out of bed and forced him to miss the most important meal of the day.

She nodded. "Fine, but you and I both know what this is going to lead to."

Darek took her hand. "Sex at my house?"

"No, silly. We have to go through Max's house. I need to make sure that there wasn't something they missed. Who knows? We might have missed an important clue."

He waited until they were alone in the elevator to give her a quick peck on the lips. "Sounds like fun. What did you say to Marvin?"

"I just wanted to see if maybe he'd open to me without you around, but it didn't work. He didn't tell me anything. I just reminded him that this is a criminal investigation and that he will continue to cooperate in the future, if not for Mia's sake, then for his."

Darek pulled her close and gave her another kiss before the elevator stopped. "That's my girl."

CHAPTER 11

BAY

Calling Lila to tell her about her sister would be one of the hardest things Bay had ever done, and like all the other difficult things he'd had to face in life, he sought counsel from Rose Marie before making a move.

She answered the phone, and her thick, rich voice gave him a calmness like no other ever could. "What is wrong?" she asked in her warm Caribbean accent.

"Now, how did you know something is wrong? And before you tell me that's the only time I call you, let me remind you that's not at all true." He had been calling the woman at least once a week or more for his entire life.

"You have to ask?" She laughed. "You should know by now that I don't have to be with you to know how you're feeling."

"I know."

"Then why don't you tell me all of your troubles?" Her voice was soothing, and he closed his eyes and imagined she was there with him.

"Mia's missing. I think she's dead."

Rose Marie didn't seem surprised, and her voice remained calm. "The old demons are coming home, aren't they? I warned you they would."

Bay never could dispute a word from the woman's mouth, and she was still the only person that had steered him straight. "Yes, ma'am. You did. But now I have to tell Lila that her sister is missing without a trace, and I'm afraid for the first time in a long time. Afraid of what it will do to her and what that will mean for the baby."

"She'll be fine. The baby will be fine." If Rose Marie said it, it was true. "She's not had any problems, Bay. But I don't think you're going to like what I have to suggest."

"You think I should have her come home," he said. "I already know I have to let her. She should be safe now, and she needs to be here, close to me. The person I was worried about is locked up. I don't think there's a threat."

Rose Marie sighed, and the sound of her breath sent chills down his spine. "You *do* know if she comes home, she'll have to stay," she said. "She won't be able to make the trip but once. Her doctor is going to agree with me. All of the back and forth, it's not good for her in the last trimester."

He gave a nod as if Rose Marie could see him. "We need to make sure she's comfortable and get her home. I want her to have the baby here. I'll make all of the arrangements to have things in order."

"I agree. And it would be my honor to help with the delivery." Bay knew that Lila wouldn't like that, but he wasn't going to tell his Rose Marie no.

"I'll arrange it. I'll beef up security here too. I'm hoping that they'll at least find Mia's body by the time she comes home. It will be easier to offer her some kind of closure. Where is her mother?"

"She's gone to the big island to chase after another man," Rose Marie said dismissively. "I don't know when she will be back, but she needs to come home as well. You know it's only right, and as much as I hate to say it, Lila will need her mother."

Bay's anger spiked, but he wasn't going to argue with Rose Marie. "She's never been a fucking mother to those girls. Lila practically raised Mia. Hell, you raised Mia more than she ever did."

"Yeah, and I hate that the precious girl is gone." Her voice was soft, and Bay thought he heard it crack.

"She is gone, isn't she?" He knew Rose Marie would know. Instinctively, she just knew things. She always had.

Rose Marie sniffled. "Let me put it this way, sugar. She's not coming back. I don't feel like we're going to see her again."

"I'm going to make sure I take care of it."

"Won't be long now and you'll be a father. You can't be taking care of things like you always did."

"Lou is dead," he said. "Someone has to do it. I'm out of options." He still had to find someone who would take care of Max in jail. He had his feelers out and expected to hear something soon. At least, he hoped.

"There are always other options, Bay. You'll listen to me one day." She paused a breath, and Bay wanted to tell her that he always listened to her. "Maybe the day your baby comes. It's going to change your heart. Awaken it. Stir something deep inside of it that only you will know. It will be a proud day for the family, and I can't tell you how excited I am that we can all celebrate that together."

"That would be nice," he said. There was so much on his mind, especially what Otis had told them about the dark-haired girl.

"I can tell there is something else bothering you, Bay. Tell me what it is so that I might ease your soul." She had always wanted to make everything comfortable for him.

"It's nothing. Just a hunch."

"You know what I'd tell you to do with a hunch."

"Trust it," said Bay. "I know. I will." His words were mostly to pacify her, but he was going to have to look into it or it would eat at him. "I'll call Lila later. I just needed to run it all by you first." He heard footsteps coming down the hall. "Someone's coming. I'll call you later."

"Okay, love. You take care." She hung up the phone, and Bay got to his feet as Lane walked into the room.

"Hey, sorry to bother you," he said. "Were you about to leave?"

Bay shook his head. "Nah, I just finished up a phone call. I'm not going out until later. I thought you'd be over at Nona's." He thought Lane was going to finish packing her things and shipping them out.

"There's too much to do and so much in my brain. I just needed a break."

Bay could tell there was something bothering him, and he wondered if it was the same thing he'd been thinking. "What's on your mind?"

"It's the woman," Lane said. "I can't get past what Otis said about his brother's girlfriend."

"You think she sounds a bit familiar too?" Bay had thought about it since they'd spoken with Gough with day before.

"Wait, you think she sounds familiar?"

"Yeah, I do. In fact, my gut tells me that we know her." He had learned from Rose Marie to always trust his intuition. She had always considered it a very powerful tool.

Lane frowned. "I was just going to suggest that maybe the girl was the first victim. Is that what you're thinking?"

"No, I think Max had help before then. Someone to help him plot out what they were doing. If you think about it, the crimes are so complex, and with Max being on the force, he had to be two places at once for a good part of the time. The only way to do that is to have a partner."

Bay had done things like that long enough to know that a good partner was important.

Lane raked his hand through his hair. His expression was wary, and Bay could tell that he hadn't been thinking the same thing. "So, who do you think it is?" he asked.

"Who is the only dark-haired beauty we know? Someone who doesn't mind a lot of kink?

"Wait, you mean Raven?" Lane's eyes widened.

"As soon as Gough mentioned her, that's who came to mind. I mean, think about it. She's been around the Zodiacs enough to know all of our moves, she's one of the only loved ones who has survived an intended attack, and she's fucked just about every one of the guys and then was friends with them at the times of their deaths. She could be the kind of person who could have told Max exactly where all of us were and when we were there."

"Damn, that's hard to believe," Lane said. "She was so nice back in New Orleans. She seems like such a good girl."

"And Max seemed like a good cop," Bay said.

Lane nodded. "I can't argue with that." He paused. "But Raven got shot at just like the rest of us. If she was working with Max, that would have put an end to it, don't you think?"

"Unless it was all part of their plan," Bay said. "A bit of misdirection. The killer couldn't possibly be someone who got shot at too, right? That's the kind of thing the killer would want us to think."

Lane look like he'd seen a ghost. "Darek's not going to like this theory."

"That's all it is. Just a theory. So, let's not go and say anything to him. I'll find out where she is and check up on her. We want to make sure she's still at Ethan's place and that she stays there. And if not, we'll need to take her out."

Lane got a panicked look in his eyes. "I don't think she'd come back to town. According to Darek, she's getting things set up for Noah."

"Well, then for the kid's sake, I hope I'm wrong. Because if he *did* witness something, maybe he's not safe either."

Lane's face fell. "Damn. That's fucked up."

"Yeah. Let's hope I'm wrong." He knew he'd have to go and find her. For her sake, he hoped that she had nothing to do with it. Then again, it might be better to be safe than sorry.

CHAPTER 12

DAREK

"We've had the worst luck today," said Lizzy as she and Darek walked out of the station. "First the damn weapon. Then Marvin was a bust, dinner was terrible, and now the press is sniffing around."

"Don't worry, baby. We got them off our ass." Darek was more worried about the press getting access to Max somehow. "I've given orders that no one gets in to see him. The reporters can try, but they won't succeed. Besides, they are way off."

The media seemed to think that a homeless man had been arrested for the murder spree, and Darek couldn't help but consider the irony.

"It's only a matter of time before they *aren't* way off, Darek. Then what?"

"Look, when that happens, we'll be ready for them. Don't sweat it in the meantime. We have to make sure we're not being tailed and get to Max's house." They would have gone earlier in the day but were called back in when the press tried to get in to see the person arrested for the Zodiac crime. Thankfully, all of the department was keeping things under wraps, but Darek had no idea how long they'd be able to keep it up.

"Fine, but can you drive again?" she asked. "I'm going to read over the file and see if there is anything from the past that might give us a clue for Mia. I pored over these papers last night but found nothing. Maybe today? Who knows?"

"Fresh eyes can't hurt. I'll drive." He took the keys, and when they got out to the car, he opened her passenger door and then went around to get behind the wheel.

After a trip across town and into the suburbs, they pulled up to Max's place. The house was about as nice as Darek's, and he parked out front, thinking about all the times he'd been there in the past. If Max had something to hide in the house, Darek would have never known it. He had never stumbled upon anything strange.

"Let's get this over with," said Lizzy. "I'm starting to think you were right. We should have just stayed home in bed this morning."

Darek smiled. "I'm telling you. One day, you'll listen to me. We could have had hot, kinky sex. Instead, we went to work. I think there's something seriously wrong with your brain, baby."

"I'll ignore that remark," she said teasingly.

They walked up to the door, and Lizzy cut through the police tape to get in. "This is a case where ladies first doesn't appeal to me," she said as she stepped aside and let Darek go inside ahead of her.

"Are you afraid of an empty house?" he asked, the teasing tone still in his voice.

She followed and then stuck her tongue out at him before she headed to Max's kitchen ahead of him. When he came in, she checked the drawers and accounted for all of Max's kitchen knives.

Darek made a pass through the laundry room. "There's nothing in here," he said, after looking around. He went back to where Lizzy stood over a counter full of knives she'd dumped from a drawer.

"Yeah, you'd think with all of these, there'd be one that looked like it could be used, but nope." She sifted through them, handling them carefully.

"I'm going into his bedroom," said Darek.

He went to the other end of the house and opened the door to Max's master bedroom. There was a hole in the wall that Darek had never seen before, and it looked like it was the size of a fist. Darek walked over and looked at it, but he wasn't convinced that it meant anything other than Max had been cracking up and losing his mind.

He dug around in some of Max's drawers, most of which were already empty due to the police search. They hadn't cleaned up after themselves, and it made it easier for Darek to see there wasn't anything to find.

Darek headed out as Lizzy walked across the kitchen floor, and she stopped short as her heels made a strange sound. "Did you hear that?" she asked.

Darek had heard the sound of something hollow beneath her feet, where Max had always had an ugly grandmother's house-looking rug. "Yeah, when you walked over here." He pointed to the area.

"The rug has been moved. Look at the faded part." Lizzy pointed out how the rug had been slid over a tad. There was a distinctly darker area where the rug had protected the floor beneath it for years. "Let's move it." She knelt down, and Darek walked over to help her roll it back. As they did, it became clear something was hidden there. "Is that a door?"

"Yeah." Darek looked at the hatch. "I never knew this was here. Max never mentioned it." He thought of all the talks they'd had about man caves and basements through their long time on the streets together. Surely, he'd have mentioned an underground room.

Lizzy opened it up and stood back. "That's a root cellar."

"What do you want to bet that's not what our friend used it for?" Darek hated to be macabre, but there was no telling what else he didn't know about his ex-partner. The man was liable not only to have Mia down there but other bodies as well. Just how big was his killing spree?

"You want to go down there first? It's full of boxes." She shined her phone's flashlight down into the hole.

"I'll go." He had to be the man and make sure all was well, although he was nervous about what he might find down there. With a sick fuck like Max, there could be anything.

Darek stepped on the first rung and hoped the ladder would hold. The house was old as dirt, and if it was part of the original construction, it could be terribly eroded. The ladder creaked, but he managed to make it down without breaking his neck.

He got to the bottom, relieved to find the entire room was in much better shape than he expected. He called Lizzy down.

"Come on, baby, it's safe." Taking special care to help her, he covered his face with his shirt. "It's pretty dank down here, but on the plus side, I don't smell the decay of human flesh."

"No," said Lizzy. She shined her phone around until she found the light and turned it on. "What is all this?"

Boxes lined the most part of the room, but there was some kind of examination table and a contraption that reminded him of some of the shit he'd seen back at the sex shop ages ago.

"Sex toys and torture devices?" Darek narrowed his eyes. "He must have been into some pretty weird shit to have all of this."

Lizzy looked grossed out at the thought of Max being into it. "That's an understatement, clearly." Lizzy let out a breath and stepped around the sex swing contraption. "I think we have to go through the boxes."

"Oh, great," said Darek. "As if I wasn't traumatized enough. I used to sit upstairs, watching TV. What if he had someone tied up down here?"

The last time Darek had been here, Max had acted a fool over Darek being in his house. He had told Darek that he had a friend coming over. Maybe they were locked up down there all along.

As Darek continued to search, Lizzy backed into a box and sent it tumbling to the floor with a crash. "Shit!" she said, covering her mouth. "That scared me."

She looked down at the stuff that had come out of the box: a bunch of leather and chains. Darek reached into the pile and held up a black leather thong with a long tail. He also found a matching mask. He had seen people wear those things at Taunt, and he had to wonder how many times he had been there when Max was there too.

"I can't imagine him wearing this," he said. "As a matter of fact, I don't want to imagine it. I think I just threw up in my mouth a little."

"Let's just hope he cleaned it after he last used it," Lizzy said.

Darek grimaced and quickly dropped the thong back on the pile. "Okay, now I definitely threw up a bit."

Lizzy turned around to another stack of boxes and found a keyring with a single key. "What's this? It was just sitting here like it wanted to be found."

Darek turned around. "Does the keychain say anything?"

She flipped over the little plastic square attached to the ring. "It's from Benny's Storage across town. I wonder what's in it."

"Only one way to find out," Darek said.

Lizzy studied the key. "There's no unit number or anything. How do we know which one is Max's?"

"We go down there and search each one?" He didn't have a better idea. Sometimes you just had to do the grunt work.

She gave Darek a defeated look. "That could take all day, and what if it's just more storage for sex shit?"

"With Mia's life on the line, we can't take any chances." He had little hope that she was still alive at this point. Even if she was tied up in one of those storage units, enough time had gone by to do her in, especially if she was bleeding or without water.

"Of course," she said. "I'm just saying it's not going to be a quick trip."

"Then let's get out of here. I don't see anything else but a cold coming on." He could feel his throat itching from the wet, moldy cellar.

"Fine." Lizzy took another step and tripped over something that clanged against the floor with a metallic sound. "Dammit." She jumped back. "Wait. Is that what I think it is?"

Darek walked over and shined his phone light on the long metal rod. "Holy shit. It's a branding iron." He looked down and saw the symbol. It was one of the unused ones, which bore Alan's symbol.

"I don't know what that symbol is," she said, narrowing her eyes at the object. "Maybe it's for another victim?"

"He must have had one for each of the Zodiac signs."

Lizzy took a few photos with her phone, and Darek found a stack of old newspapers. He grabbed one from the middle of the stack. It was still folded, and the dust hadn't touched it. He took it over and collected the branding iron. "We'll need to take this in, but I'd say it's about as close to a murder weapon as we'll get this trip."

Lizzy nodded. "Yeah, there's no denying it now. Max is our killer."

The words echoed in Darek's brain. Even though he knew that already, it still didn't seem real when he heard it. The man they'd been looking for all those months had been right under their noses. He had even taunted them with the same kind of sentiment in one of his texts to Bay. Darek wished he knew where to find that burner phone. It would hold the key to everything most likely, and then he'd know exactly what had happened to his friends without any doubts.

"I can't believe this," said Lizzy, snapping a few more images with her phone. "I think we need to get the hell out of here."

"I agree. I've seen enough." He had a horrible feeling that Lizzy would want to talk to Max about the things they'd just found. He couldn't let that happen. "Let's keep this to ourselves for a day or two, okay? We should let him think we're moving slow."

"We are," Lizzy said. "I'll be up all night at home, working on these reports. I still don't know about this key." She held it up, and Darek took it.

After a good look, he put it in his pocket. "I'll take it and see what I can find," he said. "A storage unit is a great place to stash a body. Or a murder weapon."

She shrugged. "Only if we can actually find the damn unit."

"I'll find it," Darek said. "Are you coming to my house tonight?"

She walked over to the ladder and started to climb. "You'll only distract me, Darek. I have to make notes on everything we've seen and found, and I don't want to miss a single thing."

"I'll help you remember," he said, climbing up behind her. "My mind is like a steel trap."

Lizzy made it to the top and dusted off while she waited on Darek. "You're just saying that to get me into bed, and while I find that totally intriguing, I know better."

She had turned him down a lot lately. "You know, you're starting to worry me, Lizzy. I mean, one might think that you were done with me."

"Don't be ridiculous. Why would you even say a thing like that?"

"Because you don't sleep over, and you don't want to stay and fuck. You seem to find a million excuses lately to not be with me, and I don't feel like it's all Reed's fault." He hadn't thought that Reed was ever the problem when it got right down to it.

"Darek, don't make it into something it's not." She walked to the door.

"See? You're always doing that. You duck the conversations about us." He walked out onto the stoop behind her and then shut the door, securing the police tape back into place to ward off any trespassers.

"You're way off," she said.

By the time they got to the car, he could tell that her temper was flaring, but he didn't care. "I don't think I am. Are you mad at me? Is there some kind of problem with us? Did I do something wrong?"

She let out a short breath. "As of right now, yeah, I'm getting pretty annoyed. I wonder when you'll actually start to have faith in me and in this relationship." She slid into the passenger's seat.

He hopped into the Rover. "Me? Have faith in you? Come on. Faith is all that's keeping us together, it seems. If you say we're good, I'll believe you."

"We're good." Her tone was insistent, but somehow, Darek didn't believe her. All signs pointed to no.

CHAPTER 13

BAY

The alarm on Bay's bedside table sounded a bit off, and as he went to shut it off, he realized it was because the sound was coming from his phone. He had changed the sound of Darek's ring-tone, and realizing it could be news about Mia, he sat up and quickly answered it.

"Darek? Did you find her?" He didn't mean to sound so desperate, but he was sure Darek wouldn't be brave enough to wake him up at two in the morning for anything else.

"No. Sorry, there's no word yet."

"Then why wake me up in the middle of the goddamned night? You better have a good reason." He got to his feet and walked to the bathroom to take a piss.

"I found something earlier, and I thought you'd be interested, so I didn't think it should wait."

"Then why not call me earlier?" Bay asked.

"Because I had a certain FBI agent in my bed, and I was too busy with her. She just left."

"I don't give a fuck about your love life. Tell me what the fuck it is." He didn't have time to fuck around with Darek, and he couldn't believe the asshole had waited to get his rocks off before calling. If it was something important, he was going to castrate the fucker so it never happened again.

"Lizzy and I were at Max's. We found a bunch of shit down in his basement, mostly old household goods, but there was a box of sex toys, and we found a branding iron there. It was Alan's Taurus one."

Bay let that sink in. "Well, that's good news, isn't it?"

"Yeah, especially since the knife we found in his house came back clean."

Bay gritted his teeth. That wasn't the best news of the day. "Well, at least you have enough to keep him locked up." It would probably be easier for Bay if he got turned loose. He'd put a bullet in his head before he made it to the first car.

"Yeah, believe me," said Darek. "I'm just as frustrated about that as you."

Darek had no idea how he felt. "Somehow, I doubt it. You know where Lizzy is. You're not in my shoes, so don't pretend you are." The cop was getting on his last nerve. They should have found Mia by now.

"Right, sorry," Darek said. "You're absolutely right, man. I didn't mean it that way. I did find something else; a key to a storage down at Benny's."

"Well, what did you find in the fucking unit?" There had to be something in there. A clue, evidence, something to make it worth calling him up in the middle of the night.

Darek cleared his throat. "Um, nothing yet. The problem is, no one is there, and we don't have the number for the unit. Lizzy and I are going down first thing in the morning."

Bay wanted to scream. He did the next best thing. He lashed out. "Holy hell, Darek. Do you literally have shit for brains? You should be there looking for Mia! Instead, you went back to your place for a quickie?" Bay wanted to cave in Darek's skull with his fist.

"Without the number for Max's unit, we'll need a warrant to check them all," Darek said. "That's the proper procedure, and Lizzy will be involved with the search."

Bay raised his voice. "So, get a fucking warrant, moron! You call and wake up the fucking judge. Not me!"

"You're not listening to me, Bay," Darek said. "Going through the proper channels means every cop in the department will be at the scene when we open up Max's storage unit. Which could have anything in it. Like evidence linking us directly to all of this."

Bay growled in frustration. "If you have a point, fucking get to it already."

"Jesus, Bay. My point is that we can't let that happen. We need to check this shit out first before the department does. Do you want to go with me or not? That's why I called."

"Oh, well thanks a fucking lot for telling me that in the first place," Bay said.

"You're fucking welcome," Darek said. "I'm down the street from your house. Meet me outside."

"Fine." Bay hung up and quickly got dressed in dark clothing. Even though he was angry with Darek, Bay's thoughts were focused on what Max might be hiding in his storage unit. Had he stored enough evidence to pin the Zodiacs to the wall if something happened to him? Or did the unit hold Mia's remains?

He reset the house alarm when Darek drove up. Then he went out and got into the car. "How fast does this thing go?" he asked.

"It's not as fast as your fancy car, but it's fast enough. I don't want to draw any attention to us if we don't have to."

Darek's shitty car certainly wasn't going to draw any attention. "What if Mia's in that unit? You can't get there fast enough." It wasn't that he had any hope, but Darek's blasé attitude was about to make him lose his mind.

Darek put the pedal down and didn't let off until they exited the freeway on the other side of town. "When we get there, we'll have to talk to the night guard. Explain to him what we're doing and why we didn't want to wait until morning to do things through proper channels."

"I have enough money in my wallet to get us in," said Bay. Money had always gotten him anything he wanted.

Darek rolled his eyes. "My badge works a lot of magic on its own."

Bay gave him a blank look. "Well, it must be nice to get by so cheap in life. At least that piece of metal is good for something." Bay was in a shitty mood, and he had a feeling it was only going to get worse.

When they got to the gate, Darek shut off the car. "I hope you feel like walking. We'll be lucky to get in, but I don't think the car is getting past that gate without a warrant."

"Where is this night guard?" He looked off into the distance. The units stretched on for what seemed like a mile or more.

"I'd guess he's over there." Darek pointed to the tiny guard shack, but when they walked over, the place was empty. "Well, looks like I'm wrong."

"Fuck it. We'll have to deal with him when we find him." Bay walked over to the gate and took out a lockpick kit. "I got this from a good friend of mine. I guess I can consider it my inheritance from old Lou."

"Sorry about Lou. I know you guys went way back." Darek sounded sincere, but Bay knew that Lou being on the wrong side of the law made him nothing but a casualty to Darek; one more thug off the street. To Bay, the meatball-loving old man was family.

"Yeah, if Lou were still around, we'd have already found Mia, and Max would have a slug in his skull. I'd be a happy man." Bay jimmied the lock and then slid the gate open enough to get them inside.

"Where do you want to start?" Darek asked.

"Let's split up. You take that row, and I'll take this one. We'll make our way around."

"Text me if you run into the guard. I'll bring my badge." Darek gave a smug grin.

Bay patted his pocket. "Don't worry, officer. I've gotten by without a badge for years." He didn't think Darek needed to know about the gun in his pants. That was something he usually had on him that he kept to himself. He was used to being discreet, and Darek would only know about it if he needed to use it.

Bay walked away and went down his row. He carefully listened at each one, knocking softly and calling Mia's name. When he rounded the corner at the end of the row, he saw Darek had run into a bit of trouble.

Bay pulled his gun and walked out into the opening. "Don't move," he said.

Darek breathed a sigh of relief. "I tried to tell him I'm a cop."

The guard held his gun on Darek, and Bay kept his trained on the old man, who looked like he was about to shit his pants. "I don't want no trouble," he said. "You two ain't got no business here."

"I guess you didn't get a chance to reach for that badge of yours." It was Bay's turn to give Darek a smug look.

"He's really a cop?" The security guard did not lower his weapon as he asked. He wasn't going to give either one of them the easy shot at him.

"Yes, you old bastard," Bay said. "He's a shitty cop, but a cop nonetheless."

The old guard still looked skeptical. "And who the hell are you?" he asked Bay.

Bay shrugged. "I'm the grim fucking reaper, old man. If you don't put that gun away."

Darek was growing increasingly irritated. "I'm a detective. If you lower that weapon, I'll show you my badge." Darek kept his eyes focused on the muzzle of the man's gun.

The old man's eyes narrowed. "I'll lower it, but don't you make any sudden moves, or I'll bust a cap in your ass." Bay knew he meant it, even though he was shaking like a leaf.

Darek still had a chip on his shoulder. "This wouldn't be a problem if you had been in your shed."

"I had to take a shit," said the old man. "And you know you ain't supposed to be lurking around here in the night. Coming through my locked gate."

Darek put his hand down and reached into his pocket to show his badge. "We have a key. We're looking for a missing person, and we wanted to check the unit, but we don't have a number."

The old man looked at the badge and then looked at Bay. "Tell your friend to put down his gun."

Tired of wasting time, Bay put his gun away, and the old man did the same.

"Look, is there any way to find out which lock that key goes to?" Bay asked.

"No, not unless you want to go into the office and look through the computer. But you'd need a warrant and the password for that."

"Shit," said Bay, raking his fingers through his hair.

The old man spat on the ground and then gave him a sideward look like he might know something. "I can tell you how to find the name, but you'll have to check each unit. It could take you all night."

"Someone's life is on the line," said Bay. "We'll do whatever it takes."

The old man walked them over to the nearest unit. "Look here. This label is on every unit. There is the number of the transaction, and this is the name of the person who registered it."

Bay reached into his pocket and took out his wallet, pulling out two crisp hundreds. "Here, take this for your troubles, and we'll just take a look."

The old man took the bills. "Take all the time you need." He put the money in his pocket. "I'll be in my shed if you need me." He strolled away in a much better mood than when Bay found him.

"There you go," Bay said. "He's not going to be any trouble, and we can stop worrying about getting shot."

"You didn't tell me you had a gun."

"You didn't tell me you didn't. What kind of cop—"

Darek pulled his gun out of his pants. "I didn't have time to pull it or my badge."

"Some cop you are." He shook his head, and the two of them went on their way, checking the units.

After a bit of time, Bay stumbled upon the name Gough. "Over here," he called.

Darek, who was a unit away, hurried over. "Did you find something?" He handed Bay the key and put it in the lock. When it turned and the lock came open, Bay breathed a sigh of relief.

79

"Fuck yeah. This is it." He pulled the door open, and the stench of something rotten hit them in the face. "That's not good."

He took out his phone and hit the flashlight. The place illuminated enough for him to find the light switch. The fluorescent light buzzed and flickered on, and Bay took a few steps back, seeing the blood on the floor. "Fuck!"

CHAPTER 14

DAREK

The floor was covered with dried blood and maggots, and the stench in the air was enough to trigger Darek's gag reflex at least once. Whatever Max had done there, it had been done days ago.

Bay's face had gone as pale as his hair, and Darek wondered if something had finally gotten to him.

"I'll look around," Darek said. "You might not want to see what's here to find."

He walked to the back of the storage unit, which had tons of furniture and a lot of old boxes. Some were open, their contents scattered on top of the other boxes. There was a place in the back where the blood had gotten thicker, and Darek's suspicions were that it wasn't really from a human.

"Something isn't adding up. Either he slaughtered three or four people, or this blood was deliberately put here for us to find. The key was probably a set up too. Lizzy found it sitting right on top of a box. The blood is so old. Max could have done it before we picked him up."

"What's this guy's fucking problem? He's leading us in circles and wasting our fucking time." Bay looked down at his shoes. "Fuck." The soles were stained with the thick mush.

"He's trying to fuck with us." Darek walked over to one of the boxes, filled with dildos. "Look at this shit. The man's worse off than I ever imagined."

"He's telling us to go fuck ourselves," said Bay. "That's all this is. One big head fuck. He's probably laughing right now and hoping we found it. He hasn't got any fucking intention of telling us where she is. I want you to let me talk to him."

Darek shook his head. "If he's not going to tell us, then why bother? You just want to take a crack at him, and I'm not letting you fuck everything up now. If you do that, he wins."

"Fuck that!" Bay didn't like the idea of anyone else beating him. "He won't win. He'll end up with a fucking bullet or a shank, but he won't win!" Bay pointed his finger at Darek, jabbing it in his direction like he wanted to poke an eye out.

Darek sighed. "Okay, I get it. But I can't give you the opportunity to take him out, and that's all there is to it." Bay was likely to rile Max up so much that he went to Lizzy with the truth. Why he hadn't sung his song already was a mystery, but Darek knew he was waiting for the right time. The last thing he needed was Bay going in and making things worse.

Bay walked over to one of the boxes. "Maybe there's another clue. There has to be something here, just like there was at his house." He turned out another box, this time finding a pair of fur-lined handcuffs and a box of women's clothing. "Looks like the asshole really did have a woman in his life."

"What are you talking about? He's never had a steady chick. As long as I've known him, he's had a variety of women. They never last, but—"

"No, I know he's had someone," Bay said. "A dark-haired beauty, according to Max's brother. Someone who really likes the shit he's playing with. All of this kinky shit? It's just what she likes. I'm guessing," he picked up a skin-tight, black rubber body suit, "this is hers."

"What are you talking about?" Darek asked.

"His brother told Lane and me that he used to hang with a young, emo chick. She had black hair and looked drop-dead gorgeous. Who does that sound like to you?"

"Fuck, I don't know." He shrugged, and it took a moment, but he realized what Bay was getting at. "Wait, you think *Raven* is the girl?" Bay had been rather hard on him about Raven lately, and he was getting sick of it.

"Come on. Dark hair, sexy, into kinky shit? Not to mention, she's been in this for a while and managed to come out of it alive."

The poor girl had been through hell, and Darek wasn't about to put her through any of it again. Blood rushed to his head so fast, he didn't know what he was doing. He grabbed Bay by his shirt and slammed him through the boxes, pushing him up against the wall. Before Darek could draw back his fist, he took a punch to the face. His own fist then swung out but missed his intended target as Bay ducked.

While Darek's bell rung, Bay pushed him back and broke free of his grip. "What the fuck? You know that fucking whore has been in the thick of things since this began. She was with Finn, for fuck's sake. She was with Seth, and you know she was right there on the tail end of his death! You're going to lash out at me over that cunt?"

Darek held his jaw. He had to give it to Bay. The man had a hell of a right hook. "You don't fucking know her! Do you think that just because you run that fucking club she loves so much, that it means you have a clue? You're fucking mistaken."

Bay's chest heaved with anger, and his eyes were wild. Darek could see the gleam of disbelief in them like he didn't understand what was happening. "You're thinking with your heart and your dick, which is exactly what she wants you to do. Think about it, Darek. She played you. Why do you think she wanted out? You were getting too close and fucking things up."

"You're wrong." He wasn't going to hear it. Bay was out of his mind. He'd always been jealous that she was the one girl that he could never have.

"No, I don't think I am." Bay took a breath. "Look, it's worth checking into. That's all I'm getting at. You're still close to her, whether you want to admit it or not. You still have feelings, and I'm

83

betting that you still have contact, so I'd try and find out what she's up to if I were you."

"She's still in Tennessee." Darek had just spoken with her a few days ago. She'd missed Noah's meeting, and that wasn't because she was doing anything shady. She was trying to make a better life for Noah and taking care of Ethan. "She's burying our friend."

"And for all we know, she had something to do with his death too. Where was she when Ethan died? She wasn't at the table."

"She was with Lizzy and Mia!" Darek couldn't believe him. He knew that Raven was never alone at the fucking fashion show.

"Yeah, exactly. She had gone to the bathroom, right? That could have been a signal. A way to keep Lizzy busy." It all made sense, except for the part where Raven was involved.

"You're way off. And fuck you for saying this about her."

Bay searched his eyes. "You're fucking pathetic. You *are* in love with her, aren't you?"

The words burned with anger inside him. "I have respect for her, yeah. There's a difference."

Bay held his arms out. "Well, if I'm wrong, I'll apologize, which is something I rarely do, but I have a hunch about this. I think I'm right, so I'm willing to gamble."

"Why would there be someone else?" Darek would never believe she had anything to do with it.

"Come on. You know you've thought about it before. This killing spree? Being orchestrated and carried out by one person? You know it's ridiculous. He was too busy being a cop most of the time. And he did have help. We know that. He had Alicia David."

"How do we know she's not the one his brother told you about? Maybe he had help at the start, but this is all him. Max would be too proud to have a woman as a partner in crime."

"I don't think she was a partner," Bay said. "I think she's the mastermind."

Darek couldn't help but think of how smart she was, but that wasn't going to sell him on the whole idea of it. "That's a huge stretch, Bay."

"She's used to luring men with sex. Why would this be any different?"

"Fuck this place," Darek said. "I'm sick of hearing this shit, and I want to go. It's not like we'll find Mia here. And before you mention more about me and Raven, get your facts straight. I am in love with Lizzy. I want to marry her and have a family with her. Raven had her chance, and she bailed on me."

He realized what he'd said, what he'd been angry about all along. Raven had abandoned him. He had loved her, and she'd just taken off. He was never going to forget that as long as he lived; the way it made him feel; the way it had hurt. It was so different than the way he'd loved Megan or Lizzy. But now, he was a lucky man. Lizzy had taken him back, and he wanted to focus on his life with her. It was the right thing to do.

No matter how many times he tried to convince himself of it, it just never sat right.

"Convince yourself all you want," Bay said. "Hell, for your sake, if I'm right, I hope you really do love Lizzy. You'd be better off. But I don't think I'm wrong." Bay straightened his shirt and then gave Darek a push on the shoulder. "If you ever pull shit like that again with me, I'll feed you your teeth, and I won't let up until there's nothing left of you. Your blood will be on this goddamned floor, attracting flies. Are we clear?"

Darek's face grew warm. "Don't threaten me, Bay. I've tried to work with you on this case, to save both of our asses, but don't think that makes me weak. Don't mistake me for that weak fucking kid you met back at camp. That's not me, and Raven is not in this with Max. I'd know."

"Trust me," Bay said. "If I still thought of you like that little asshole who was afraid of his daddy, this would be ending a whole lot different. I'd have never expected you to help any of us."

Darek wanted to tell him to look around. The others were dead, only they and Lane remained. He hadn't done anything extraordinary.

Even though part of him wanted to hate Bay for what he had suggested about Raven, a part of himself worried he was right. The things he'd said about Raven were horrible, but that didn't mean it wasn't a good theory. What would be her motive, though? She had it all, and he couldn't see her wanting Max so much that she'd do anything for him.

Darek gathered some of the blood for testing, and they left the storage unit. He hurried out to the car, ready to get Bay home, and then he was going to check on Raven and make sure she was where she said she was.

It seemed like every time he tried to tell her goodbye for good, something else would come up, and he'd find himself calling her again. She was an old wound, and Darek wasn't sure if it would ever heal.

CHAPTER 15

BAY

With the blood sample still being analyzed, and no doubt pushed to the back of the pile, Bay wasn't going to sit around and do nothing. Knowing Lila was on her way, he had to make every effort to find Mia's body. He hired a diving team to comb the river behind the storage buildings.

As the wind blew through his hair, he watched from the shore, and he was shocked when Lane came up behind him. "I thought you were at Nona's."

Lane nodded. "Yeah, I'm on my way back. I went out for food and thought I'd come out and see if you were okay." With that, Bay gave him a sideward look. "I mean, like, if they found anything."

"Nothing yet. They've been at it for a few hours. They said she might have been dragged farther down by the current. I'll have them look for another couple of days."

"So, you didn't get anything back about the blood?" Lane asked.

"No." He sighed. "Just more waiting."

"You should call Darek and ask him to check on it."

"Darek is on my shit list," Bay said. "He tried to fight me last night. I hit him so hard his teeth rattled." He should have knocked them out.

The man had taken him by surprise with his attack, but Bay figured it was a long time coming.

Lane seemed shocked. He put his hands in his pockets and looked out over the water. "Fuck, are you two okay? I mean, you're not still pissed, are you?"

"Nah, and I don't give a fuck if we aren't. I can't help it if the man can't handle the idea that Raven might be involved."

Lane's eyes widened. "Fuck. You told him that theory?"

Bay nodded. "It's a theory, but a damned good one."

"Wow." Lane rattled the change in his pocket. "I might just stay at Nona's tonight. I know you said Lila should be home. I'll give you guys some privacy."

Bay didn't mind him being around. Lane was no trouble, and he had been there for him and Mia after the shooting. "You can come and stay whenever you like. You're not going to bother us."

About that time, the divers came to the surface, and the man who was in the boat looking at the depth finder hollered at Bay. "We're having trouble with the currents. It's all muck and mess out there. Our visibility is shot. We could try again in a few hours, see if the wind dies."

"Wrap it up and continue later. You can come back tomorrow." Bay had paid the men a small fortune for the search, and they were eager to return to make more money.

"We'll give it another try, thanks." He watched the men begin to come to shore.

"I'm going to go," said Lane. "If you need something, call me." Lane's hand clapped him on the back, and then the man stepped away.

Bay took out his keys and walked to his car. He had to get home. Lila was due there soon, and he didn't want to miss her arrival.

He drove across town and was shocked to see that Lila had made it home early. Her bags were still downstairs, and Rose Marie met him at the door, greeting him with a kiss. "How was your trip?" he asked her.

"It was good, and Lila did okay. She's upstairs. I was just about to call you. We got in a little earlier than we expected. Lila had the times mixed up. I didn't realize it until we landed."

"It's okay," Bay said. "I guess I should go up and talk to her."

"Yeah," said Rose Marie. "She needs to know. It's her sister."

Bay thought of all the times the two of them had butted heads, but in the end, they loved each other. With all the drama and all the jealousy, they were really two of a kind, sisters to the end. That end was now.

He kissed Rose Marie, and she walked him to the staircase. Bay took a deep breath and headed up. There was no way around it. He had to tell her.

Walking down the hall, he was headed to his master bedroom but found Lila standing in Mia's room.

"Darling!" she said, turning around. "I was just looking at Mia's handiwork. It's not too bad if you like this Pepto-Bismol, dismal color."

He walked into the room, and she met him halfway.

"It's her favorite," Bay said. Lila's taste in color was more like champagne and white. She had paled out the entire house when they moved in.

"Well, I want to paint our bedroom now. What do you think?"

Bay put his hands on her baby bump. "You're too pregnant for the fumes, and I'm not hiring anyone to do it. Mia did this herself."

"Mia? Well, maybe I could get her to paint ours. Where is the little fiend?"

"I need to talk to you about Mia," he said.

"If I bought her a new handbag, I bet she would do the painting for me. Unless you've already gotten her so spoiled that she doesn't want to help her big sister anymore."

Bay had made them kiss and make up since their last fight, and while they'd come to an understanding, Lila still didn't know that he was sleeping with her little sister.

"Lila, I think we should sit down." Bay took her hand and walked her to the bed.

"I don't want to sit in here. Let's go to our room. We can cuddle."

"Lila." He was trying to be patient with her.

"You don't want to cuddle with me and the baby? Is it because I'm too fat?" Her face twisted into a mask of pain and hurt, and Bay let out a breath, knowing he needed to handle her with kid gloves, which wasn't his usual nature.

"You're beautiful, and you're not fat. You're pregnant. There's a big difference."

"Am I the prettiest pregnant woman you've ever seen?" she asked.

"Yes, without a doubt." He meant it too. He might want to choke her out most of the time, but there wasn't anyone more beautiful than Lila. Not even Mia could pull that off. "But I need you to prepare yourself for some horrible news, Lila. I'm afraid that something terrible has happened."

She searched his eyes, and hers lit with horror as if she suddenly saw how serious he was. "What is it? Where's my sister, Bay?"

"I'm not sure." He raked his hand through his hair and carefully chose his words. "She's been missing for days now."

"Oh," Lila said, sounding relieved. "She's probably at her friend's house or with a man. You know how she can be. Did you upset her, Bay?"

Bay shook his head. "No, it's not like that. She was taken by someone who was arrested for murdering another girl. I'm worried she's been murdered, too."

Lila's face twisted with dread. "Oh, Bay. You're not serious? This is a joke or a bad dream."

He knew she was going to have a true meltdown if he didn't take control. "Kitten, I need you to stay calm. Being upset won't help the baby, and it won't bring Mia back to us."

She began to wail, her tears pouring down her cheeks and her feet giving out beneath her. Bay scooped her up, and though she was big with his child, she was still light as a feather, her tiny frame limp in his arms. He carried her to their room, and when he entered the hall, Rose Marie stood in the stairway, tying knots in a string. He knew she was busy doing some kind of spell, and he hoped that whatever it was for, it would keep his child safe.

"Oh, Bay, we have to tell my mother. I don't know what we'll do without Mia. She can't be gone. She's a survivor, Bay. She always was, you know?" Lila continued to ramble, and Bay let her talk. She was shaking and beside herself, and he wasn't sure what to do for her.

"Rose Marie?" he called, but Lila shook her head.

"No, don't call her in here. I don't want her to see me like this." She began to wipe her eyes.

"Calm down. I'll have Rose Marie get you something to rest your mind."

Lila shook her head. "No! No! Keep her away from me with her voodoo magic. She's crazy."

Rose Marie waved him over, and though he didn't want to leave her there, he walked across the room to where Rose Marie waited by the window. "She's distraught. She doesn't mean it."

"Please, she means it, and that's fine too. I don't need everyone to like me, Bay. I can make her some tea to calm her nerves, but you're going to have to lie to her and tell her it came from the doctor. She doesn't trust me like you do."

Bay looked at Lila, who hid her face with the pillow. "I'll do whatever you think is best," he told Rose Marie. "She's taking it a lot harder than I expected."

He didn't know what to do for her, and this was one of those times he was glad to have Rose Marie in his life. She could take care of Lila and the baby, if Lila would only let her.

Bay went back to Lila as Rose Marie turned and left. "You're going to be fine," he said. "I've instructed her to call the doctor."

"She's a witch, Bay. I don't want her to come near me with that nonsense."

"Would I ever let anything happen to you, Kitten? You're my girl, and that's my baby. You need to trust me and trust her. She loves you."

Her eyes were wild. "She loves you, she loves the baby, but she doesn't love me. I want my sister."

"I know. I do too, and I'm working on finding her."

"Are the police looking for her?" Her eyes were so clear and green, and he wished that he could tell her that they were, but instead, he wanted her to take it easy.

"Lie down, baby. Let your mind rest, okay."

"I can't. I can't do it. Not while Mia is out there. I need to find her. I need my little sister, Bay. I can't live in a world where she's not a part of it." She held her stomach and then her mouth. "I think I'm going to be sick."

She scrambled to her feet and hurried to the bathroom, where he heard her retch as soon as she disappeared behind the door.

Bay gave her some space and went to find Rose Marie. He made it halfway down the stairs, but she was already walking up from the bottom with a cup of tea. "This should settle her down and calm her stomach. Have her sip it slowly."

How the woman knew she was sick to her stomach was beyond him, but he thanked her, took the tray, and walked back into the bedroom. He found Lila standing in the doorway of the bathroom, resting against the jamb. "Come on, Lila. Let's get you into bed."

She looked up at him with a look of hopelessness. "Bay." With that, she held her stomach and swayed on her feet.

"Lila!" Bay ran across the room and made it just in time to catch her before she hit the floor. He looked up and saw Rose Marie standing in the doorway. "Call nine-one-one!" No matter how much he believed in Rose Marie's magic, she couldn't help them now. He gathered Lila up in his arms and hurried downstairs. He had to get her help. He couldn't lose two people he loved, much less three.

CHAPTER 16

LANE

Lane had finally made a dent in Nona's belongings. While he had more items to donate, the shipping costs for the things he felt he needed to send to Aunt Mary were going to be through the roof. He never knew Nona was so sentimental, but she'd kept every single thing he'd ever given her, including his phone number, which was scrawled on a bar napkin.

That, he put into his wallet, along with a gum wrapper from their first date.

Her murder had taken place in the closet, so some of her clothes had been tossed out during the cleaning process, but many others needed to be taken off the hangers and folded. Not to mention the things in the guest closet, which was just as full. She had a shopping habit that had nearly landed her in hot water on her rent more than once, and Lane, not wanting her to lose the apartment that he'd once rented as his own, had bailed her out every single time.

In many ways, it was as if the two had been married all along, and it only made him angry with himself to think about how he'd treated her when she'd wanted to make it official. If she'd only told him that she'd spoken to Aunt Mary about them, then maybe he'd have taken the whole thing a lot more seriously.

Instead, she'd chosen to tell him about her friends and how their recent engagements had influenced her. Maybe she was afraid to put her heart out there before seeing his reaction. Maybe she didn't want him to see the soft center of her soul that she'd always tried so hard to hide behind her brash exterior. But he'd always known it was there, or else he'd never had put up with her shit for all those years. He gave a half-hearted laugh thinking about how something as simple as a gum wrapper had given her away in the end.

He filled another box with her shoes, including her favorites which she jokingly called her hooker heels. They were his favorite, too, mostly because she'd keep them on during sex. He looked at the stiletto heels and remembered how she'd nearly taken his eye out by putting those babies on his shoulders.

At least his mood was light, and that was a relief. He had spent too many hours with a sick feeling in his gut; too many with tears running down his face; too many with the thought that he'd never love again weighing him down.

He thought of how she wouldn't want him to break down. She'd call him a pussy and tell him to suck it up.

He felt the lump form in his throat, and he decided to drown it out. He went to the mini bar she kept in her living room. The TV was still on from his last break, and it was nice to have a little bit of noise to keep him from getting lost in his head for too long. He poured himself a drink and then plopped into the nearest chair to stare at the screen.

The vibration in his pocket startled him. "Son of a—"

He was so jumpy. He felt like a dumbass as he looked at his phone. The number wasn't one he recognized, but he answered it anyway, not knowing if it was someone from the funeral home. "Hello?"

"Is this Lane Simon?"

Lane recognized the voice right away. "Otis Gough?"

"Yeah, I found your card in my toolbox." He gave a quiet laugh. "I had to wait until my wife went to work to call you. She's not big on me being involved, but there were a few things eating at me."

"I'm glad you called," Lane said. "Feel free to say whatever. I know it was probably a shock to have two strangers show up, asking about your family, and especially telling you about your brother. We weren't sure if you knew or not. We actually thought he might have called you from jail."

His pulsed raced, wondering what was on Otis's mind. He hoped that he would get some kind of information that could lead to Mia. He reached into a drawer on the end table and found Nona's unicorn tablet and pen. She had always used it to write down her takeout orders, but Lane needed it in case the man said something that he needed to remember.

"Yeah, well you'd be surprised. When your father is falsely accused of murder, you get all kinds of crazies at your door. Lately, we've had a lot of people showing up to make docuseries. They're really popular. We've turned down every offer. I will not have my father's name dragged through the mud again. Besides, my wife is trying to get Netflix's attention. She says the kids should have a college fund, so I'm holding out, I guess."

Lane couldn't judge them. They'd been through a lot, and thankfully, whatever story they'd have to tell, it wouldn't tell the true side of things. At least, he hoped. "Yeah. So, what was on your mind?"

"I was just wondering what will happen to my brother, I guess."

"I wouldn't expect him to get out anytime soon, but other than that, I have no idea. You won't have to worry about the death penalty here in New York, but if they find that he's guilty of crimes in another state, then that might come on the table. Especially if the other state works hard enough to get him moved."

"He's going to die in prison either way," said Otis. "I guess I just have to face that. That's the bottom line. Just like the old man."

"Except your brother is guilty." Lane didn't realize what his words would mean to the man.

"You don't believe my father was guilty?" Otis asked.

"I didn't look at the case, and it's not for me to judge." He didn't know what to say, other than that.

He thought of what he'd told Lizzy. The pedophile story was only to pacify her from making a connection to the Zodiacs, but he still felt like shit about it. He wondered what the man would think of him if he knew what he'd said about his father, and he got an aching emptiness in his gut because of it.

"I've only been looking into the disappearance of a friend," Lane said.

"The girl," said Otis. "She's another reason I called you. I couldn't get her out of my head. She reminded me so much of Emily Johnson. I felt like an ass for not being able to help more. Have you found her?"

"No, not yet. We fear that she's dead at this point. She's been missing for five days now. Six if you count the day she went missing. We just don't know where to look and had hoped that you knew your brother's habits enough to give us a lead."

"I thought you were a cop, but your card says you own a restaurant? In New Orleans?" He'd given him a card from his restaurant with a half-price beer coupon.

"Yeah, I'm not a cop. I'm in town because someone, maybe your brother, killed a friend of mine." He didn't know if he should tell the man he used to be a lawyer or not.

"I'm sorry for your loss," Otis said. "I haven't had much luck with the police, as you probably know. So, I wasn't sure what to say. I don't know of any places outside of Virginia that my brother might have an attachment to. It's where we lived with my stepmom when Dad left. Our real mother had moved to Tennessee, but she died a couple of years ago."

Lane thought of Raven being in Nashville. That connection was only a coincidence because of Ethan, but then Lane wondered about the connection. "You mentioned a girlfriend. The one you kicked out with your brother."

"Yeah," he said. "That girl came out of nowhere. They hit it off overnight, it seemed."

"You don't remember her name?" Lane didn't want to bring Raven's name up unless necessary.

"No, I'm not sure he ever used it in front of me. He just called her 'baby.' You know? Baby this and baby that. I was only around her for a day. As soon as we saw what was going on in our basement, my wife tossed him and his *baby* out on their asses."

"I can't blame you." He needed to make the most of the call and decided to ask a few questions. "Did you ever know anything about the girl your father was said to have killed?"

"No, once I learned about her, she was dead, so there wasn't anything left to know."

"I mean, did she have a sibling? A sister or a brother? Someone close to her, other than her dad?"

"Her dad? Damn, that man was a real piece of work. I always wondered about him because Emily *did* have a sister. I wondered if he—"

"A sister?" Lane blurted out the question, and though his pulse raced, he needed to make sure that he didn't spook Otis into ending the call.

"Yeah, and since he was so hard on Emily, I wondered if the other girl got the same treatment. I know they talked about removing her from the house, but I don't think they ever did."

"How come that's not in any of the records?" Lane realized his slip. "I looked into the records to find your brother."

"Oh, yeah, they didn't let the press involve her. She was a minor at the time like me, and since she was traumatized by her sister's death, they cut her a break. At least, it seemed that way."

"But you're sure she was Emily's sister?" Lane asked.

"Oh yeah, I'm positive of that. She never came to court, but I met her at a preliminary hearing. It was the only one she attended. Her father talked to her like she was some kind of dog, and she left after only a little time. She was one of those girls who hid behind her hair."

"Yeah, well, considering what happened in her life and what you're telling me, I can imagine." Lane wondered if she could she be the emo chick. Could she have been a young Raven? He would have to find out, and now that he knew she existed, it would be a hell of a lot easier to look for her in the records.

He had a lot of work to do, and still so much to do for Nona, but he let the man talk as long as he wanted. Although over the next twenty minutes, he didn't really have anything that topped Emily's sister.

Finally, Otis let out a long breath. "Well, I guess I should get out there and fix my bike. Sorry again for the other day. I wish I could help you with your friend. I hope they find her alive and well."

Lane knew the chances of that were slim. "Thanks." They ended the call, and he fell back against the couch. He had to call Kenneth Warner, but he would call Bay first.

He dialed Bay's number.

"Hey," he answered. "I can't talk right now. I'm at the hospital."

"Is everything okay?" Lane asked.

"Lila didn't take the news about Mia very well. She's okay. The stress induced some pain, but she's fine otherwise. They have her and the baby being monitored." Lane could hear the sound of the monitor in the background, and the sound was like that of a galloping horse. Bay's little one sounded strong. "I'll call you back. The doctor's here."

The phone went dead before Lane had a chance to tell him anything. He went through his contacts and found the number for Kenneth Warner.

CHAPTER 17

BAY

Bay had been so worried about the baby when Lila collapsed that he scared himself. Never had he experienced that rush of emotion, not even when taking another man's life. Was it true, what Rose Marie had said about the baby awakening something within him? Would he go soft hearted, as Lane had said, and end up some weak-minded fool on the floor pushing cars around and making stupid sounds with his lips?

Fuck that.

With the doctor ordering an ultrasound, he had learned that he was going to have the son he'd always wanted, so he wasn't going to start acting like a pussy. He had a kid to influence, a little mind to sculpt. He had to watch his every move.

He gripped Lila's hand tightly as he tucked his phone away and listened to the doctor say a lot of big words. "The little fella is going to be just fine, and you, little mama, I'd suggest you take it easy too. I think it might be best to do as little physical work as possible and stay off your feet."

"I don't do anything as it is, Doctor Walsh." Lila's voice was still scratchy and weak from crying for Mia. She hadn't stopped since she woke up, not even when the ambulance got her to the hospital. "But my baby sister is missing."

Dr. Walsh's eyes widened. "Did you say missing? As in a missing person?" He looked at Bay.

Bay nodded. "Yes, that's what I wanted to talk to you about. She's been in severe distress since learning this hours ago. Is there anything we could do for her to calm her nerves?" He knew she wasn't going to take well to Rose Marie's herbal remedy.

"I can prescribe something to help her sleep. Sometimes, sleep is the best medicine, and in her case, she's going to need something to help ease her mind." He stepped up and patted Lila's hand. "Stay strong for the baby." Then he turned his eyes up at Bay. "I'd like to speak with you in private, Mr. Collins."

The doctor stepped away, and Bay followed.

"Do you know what happened with the sister?" the doctor asked. "Did she run away?"

"No, we fear she's dead. The police are involved, but I had to tell Lila. Now, I wish I'd kept my mouth shut about it."

Dr. Walsh shook his head and patted Bay on the shoulder. "No, you did the right thing. She needs to know, but I will advise that she not suffer any further stress from details. Whatever the outcome, the meds will make sure she's sleeping. Don't worry. I wish you all luck with the situation."

"Thanks, Doc." Bay shook the man's hand and then went back into the room. Lila was lying so still, he thought she was sleeping. Her small frame was out of proportion with her huge belly, and it made her seem more fragile.

Rose Marie was standing at the window. "Did the doctor say anything else?"

"Just that we need to keep things as low stress as possible." He gave her a knowing look. "And that he'll be giving her something to keep her calm."

"I don't see why everyone keeps saying that," Lila said. "I'll calm down when they find my sister."

Bay wished she'd just cooperate for once. Even at this moment, when things were so serious, she had to make it harder. "Now is not the time to be your usual bratty self. You should at least try to think positive for the baby's sake."

"You already love him more than me," she pouted. "I'm just a vessel for the son you always wanted. I know you wish it was me instead of Mia. I know you've been sleeping with her all of these months."

Bay's temper flared, but he tried to control himself. "You should really think hard before you pick a fight with me."

"What? What are you going to do? You wouldn't hurt me. I'm the mother of your little boy."

Had she seriously gotten that comfortable? Bay felt like he'd been slipping on her discipline. She had been away from him for too long. He glared down at her. "Do you ever wonder what happened to my own mother, Lila?"

"Not now," said Rose Marie as she stepped up to the bed, her dark brown eyes hard on Lila. "You both need to mind your tongues. I'm sure that Lila here wants the best for her child, the same as you do. I'm sure she's going to close her mouth and try to sleep, being thankful that she and her baby are both safe."

Lila's face paled, and she looked away from them both.

"I'm going out to make a few calls," Bay said. "I'll be back in soon. Will you look after her?"

"You know I will." Rose Marie had always been so good to him and tolerable with Lila.

He left the room and went down the hall to a small lobby on the end. He dialed Lane's number.

"Hey, sorry I called at a bad time," he said when he answered. "I just had to tell you about the call I got."

"Let's hear it," Bay said. "I've had a stressful day, so I hope it's good."

"Oh, it's good. I found out that Emily Johnson had a sister."

"What? How come I've never heard of her before?" Bay had studied the case, and he knew that Darek had searched for enough clues that a sister would have been found at some point.

"She was a minor at the time of the murder," Lane said. "I'm guessing that child services probably had something to do with it. They will take precautions to protect children who have already been in a bad home when something horrible happens. If she had a sister murdered and the service had already formed a case, they could have stepped in."

"Makes sense, I suppose. Do we have a photograph?"

"Not yet, but I'm working on it. When I hung up with you earlier, I called Kenneth Warner. He's going to text me when he finds something. He's been really cooperative, but only because he wanted Gough's name cleared."

"Good luck with that," said Bay, feeling amused. "What are the chances that we know this girl?"

"I think she could be the girl Max was seeing," Lane said. "Maybe our theory is right. As soon as I find a photograph, we'll know."

"Then you'll let me know. I need to stay here with Lila." He wasn't going to leave her unless they found Mia. Even if she *was* a pain in his ass.

"Yeah, I'll let you know. How's the wife?"

"She's a brat, which I usually appreciate, but today, it's wearing on me. I just wish she'd settle down and sleep for my son's sake."

"Son?" Lane asked.

Bay grinned ear to ear. "Yeah, it's official. I have a son. So, you should look out. He's going to rule the fucking world someday."

"Congratulations, man. That's got to be great news."

It was nice to have someone to share the news with. "Thanks. Have you talked to Darek about the girl?" asked Bay. He wanted to be the one to tell him.

"No, not yet. I wanted to tell you first."

"If you don't mind, I'll fill him in," Bay said. "I have to call him."

"Well, tell him I said hi. I'm about to get the last boxes ready for Nona's aunt. I'm going to stay here tonight and get it done."

"Hit me later if you hear anything." Bay ended the call and looked out at the afternoon sun while he contemplated calling Darek. He was already in a shitty mood, so he might as well get it over with.

Darek answered on the first ring. "Yeah?"

"Don't sound so glad to hear from me." He hadn't expected to be the first one to call since their scuffle, but that was the way it had played out, and he didn't have much choice.

"Sorry, I'm in the middle of typing up a report. Fudging one is more like it. If you called for an apology, you're not getting one. I still don't agree with what you said, so if you called to say it again, save your breath."

"Yeah, well, I'm not either," Bay said. "You push me; you get hit. But that's not what I called about. I had to tell Lila what happened to Mia, and now she's in the hospital, so I want you to kick it into high gear."

Darek sighed. "I'm lucky every minute Max hasn't pulled the rug out from under us both, so I need you to step up *your* game. I thought you were going to find a way to take this asshole out."

"Did you hear what I just said? Lila, the mother of my child—"

"You mean your wife. Yeah, I know her. She looks a lot like her sister."

Bay's back stiffened. "Are you seriously choosing now to fuck with me? Normally, I'd be proud of you for the lack of heart, but you're poking the bear."

"Sorry, how's Lila?"

"She's okay. My son's okay, too, but she'll have to be on bedrest for the remainder of her pregnancy. I wanted you to know what was up. The minute you hear anything about Mia, I want a phone call. The sooner I can get this all behind us, the better. Lila's not going to settle down until she has closure."

"Noted," Darek said.

"Well, that's not the only reason I called. Lane got a call today from Otis Gough, Jr. He had something interesting to say about our Emily Johnson."

"Don't call her that," Darek said. "She wasn't ours like some kind of property."

"Right." Bay rolled his eyes. "But she *did* belong to someone. She had a sister. And for some reason, I didn't know about it."

"That's impossible. If she had a sister, I'd know. Lizzy and I investigated her family. She was obsessed with it."

"Well, she's as good of a detective as you, I guess. Which means that you better go over your case files again. I won't bother telling you who I think the girl is. I'll leave that to your imagination."

"I'll pretend you're talking about someone else."

The line went dead, and Bay laughed. Darek had finally grown a pair.

CHAPTER 18

LANE

After the tape was across the final box, Lane got up from his knees and dusted off his pants. He had worked hard to get everything done. With any luck, he'd be home in another week and on with his life.

As if his future was calling, his phone rang, and the name on the screen read: Jennifer. He answered. "Please tell me it's not another kitchen fire."

"Not this time, boss. But we did have a fight in the bar. A lady punched a man over his girlfriend. Knocked his dentures out of his mouth, and they went across the room and landed on the other end of the bar."

"Dentures?"

Jennifer laughed. "Yeah, they were in their eighties."

"Wow. Once again, I've missed all the fun."

"Nah, I'm lying. I just thought it might make you laugh."

Lane smiled. "You're good. And a true friend. I need a good laugh."

"Ouch," she said. "Did you just friend zone me? After all of the flirting we did last night?"

"Absolutely not. Don't get the wrong idea. I mean, yeah, I should friend zone you, you're my employee, but I just can't help myself. Besides, you started it."

"I did. I'm guilty." She laughed again, and the sound was so refreshing to him, he wished he was there with her. "So, any word on when you're coming home?"

"I just need to tie up a few loose ends, and then I'll be back," he said. "I know you can't stand to be without me."

"I can't. It's a lot easier with you around, and I think you need to heal." Her voice had fallen into a sincere but sultry tone.

"Actually, I think you're right."

"Hey," she said. "All kidding aside, I want to be here for you."

"I know, and I appreciate that. I'd like that too." He wanted her more than he could express. She was about the only good thing he had left in his life, other than his restaurant. Maybe they'd make a whole new life together.

"You know what's strange?" she asked.

He sat up straighter. "What's that?"

"I feel like I've kissed you before, even though I know I haven't. Do you get that feeling too?"

"Like we've kissed?" he asked. "I guess I can see what you mean."

They had spent some time flirting and exchanging photos on Snapchat. She'd even gone as far as showing him her tattoos and all of her piercings. That was a welcome surprise, especially since it meant he got to see her nipples. She had amazing tits, and he could feel his blood flowing just thinking about them.

"Do you promise to kiss me when you get back home?" she asked. "Or is it going to be an awkward, boss/employee kind of vibe?"

Lane knew he wanted to kiss her, especially if he was going to get to tongue those nipple rings. He had thought about it ever since she showed them to him. "Yes, of course. I promise I'll kiss you."

"Where?" Her voice took on a raspy tone that sent chills down his spine and made him hard.

"Where? I don't know, the kitchen?" He smiled, knowing that wasn't what she meant.

She burst out laughing. "Not the kitchen, silly. I didn't mean where, as in a place. I meant where on my body." She giggled, and Lane had to adjust himself.

"Pardon me. I guess I'm still an hour late to the party." Lane didn't know what was wrong with him. He and Nona had a good, adventurous to a degree, sex life, and it wasn't like him to blush, especially after his romp at Night Heat with the waitresses, Sunshine and Buffy. But this girl made him feel young again, and he was certain by the sting in his cheeks that he had turned a visible shade of red.

"That's okay by me, as long as you get there," she said.

"You certainly know how to distract a man." He couldn't believe how hard his cock was. "You turn me on."

"Are you turned on right now?" she asked.

"Very."

"Prove it," she said.

Lane wasn't about to send the girl a dick pic, if that was what she was getting at. He knew better. With her being his employee, she could take him for everything he had. While he hoped that wasn't her game, he didn't want hard proof lying around for some trumped-up sexual harassment case. "How do you want me to do that?"

"Touch it," she said. "I can tell by your voice if you do."

She was incredible.

"Okay, so what are you going to do?" he asked.

"I don't know, boss. What do you think I should do?"

"The same," he said, reaching his hand into his pants. "What are you wearing?"

She giggled. "A black silk blouse and a tight, black pencil skirt. I also have my hair up and a small gravy stain on my hem where some barbarian spilled his food."

Lane sighed. "You're still at work?" His voice had dropped an octave with disappointment.

"Off the clock and in your office with the door locked. Did you know that this room smells like you? Makes me want to hump your chair."

Lane belted a laugh. She was a wild child and just what the doctor ordered. "You make me laugh, Jennifer."

"You can call me Jenny, you know? I don't mind. Are you touching it yet?" The laughter in her voice matched his own.

"Not when you're making me laugh," he said, lying. His cock felt good in his hand, and it was the most attention it had gotten since he and Nona had been together. He listened to Jenny's laughter, treating it like therapy to ease his wounded heart. "Talk to me, and I might."

"I'm sitting in your chair with my feet on your desk like I'm some-body important."

"And where are your hands?" he asked, closing his eyes.

"One is on this phone, while the other is playing with my nipple ring. It gives me tingles, just like your voice."

"That's where I want to kiss you," he said, moving his hand from the base of his hard cock to the tip. "I want to tease you there and play with your rings."

"That sounds like a lot of fun, Lane. If you kiss me, would you promise that you'll let me see it?"

"I'll let you do more than see it, Jenny." He couldn't believe what was coming out of his mouth. He was fucking around with his employee, and she was at work, in his office.

"Can I show you something? On video?" She sounded like she was up to something, and Lane couldn't wait to find out what.

"Okay, sure. Call me back?"

"Yes." She hung up the phone, and a moment later, his video chat came through. "Hey there." He knew he probably looked worn out, with puffy eyes, and he hoped she wouldn't be turned off by that.

"This is much better, don't you think?" she asked. She'd placed the phone on his desk, and it was perfectly aimed at her breasts.

"Much better." Lane couldn't believe her, especially when she threw head back, closed her eyes, and began to moan. "Where are your hands?"

"Exactly where you think they are," she said. "I'll try not to ruin your chair, but I won't make any promises."

"Just for peace of mind, who is looking after the restaurant?" he asked.

"Pepe is on duty. I told him I had to make a long call to you. He's good with it, and the door is locked."

"You're a terrible employee."

"Perhaps you should punish me," she said.

He watched her hand moving between her legs. He could catch a small glimpse of her fingers making their way inside her. "I will, just as soon as I get back."

His words turned her on, and she moaned, biting her lip to keep from getting too loud. She wasn't the good girl he'd expected, and while he loved how she came on to him, he couldn't help but think of what a naughty girl she was. He had hit the jackpot, and he couldn't wait to get back to New Orleans to fuck her properly.

"I'm going to come," she said. Then she released a much louder moan, and Lane pumped his hand faster.

"Fuck, me too." His release came fast, and he somehow managed not to get it on the furniture. "Damn, I'm lightheaded."

"I can't wait until you come back home," said Jenny. She picked the phone up and then leaned in and kissed the screen. "At some point, I need to talk to you about that wedding date."

He got a text, and when he looked at his phone, he saw Kenneth Warner's name and half of a sentence from a message, asking about the fax machine.

"That sounds good," he said. "Look, I better go clean up. You've got me in a mess here." He couldn't deal with Warner like that. He would shower and see what the man wanted.

"Sorry, not sorry," she said with a giggle.

"Definitely not sorry. Only sorry that I have to get off the phone with you. Call me back later when you close."

"Will do, boss." With that, she gave a sexy goodbye and hung up.

Lane hurried to his feet, wondering what had just happened. She had come on hot and heavy. While it was a complete turn on and they had talked more lately, he wasn't sure he was ready for something with a younger woman.

Ready or not.

He went into the bathroom where he'd forgotten Nona's toothbrush in the holder. He washed his hands and then stripped down to shower. He picked up Nona's toothbrush and thought about throwing it away. But despite what he'd done, he put it back in the holder.

After a piping hot shower, which took up the next ten minutes of his night, he got out and dried off. Knowing he had more than one pair of sleep pants, he went to the bed where he'd left them and pulled a pair on. He had to add his things to his luggage for the trip home and wondered if he should just toss them in the trash.

As he was tying in his drawstring, he heard a noise. It was enough to bring his head up, but then he didn't hear anything else. He thought for a moment that he needed to check it out, but as the silence stretched on, he decided to let it go. He had let his overactive imagination get the best of him most of his life, but not tonight. He still needed to see what Kenneth Warner had messaged him about.

He went back to the living room, talking to Nona. "If you're here lingering around and haunting me, I'm sure you're pissed, but I still have needs." He sat down and found his phone where he left it. There had been another missed call, so he decided to call it back.

Kenneth Warner answered. "Sorry if I bothered you. I'm going out with the wife, and I just wanted to tell you that I found the girl. I'm not sure if you're going to know her or not. The photo is old, but the information is all there. I faxed it to that number you gave me."

Lane knew that Bay wasn't going to leave Lila's side, which meant the fax would be sitting unnoticed at Bay's house. "Oh, shit. Is there any way you could send it to my email?"

"I will later. My wife's hungry for ice cream, but I can stop off on my way back home. It might take a while. Text me your email."

"Do you have it on your phone?" Lane asked.

"No," said the old man. "Should I?"

"You can just take a photo of the photo and send it to my email. If it's faster when you swing by."

"I don't have a good camera, but I could email it. Send me your email." The old man seemed in a hurry, and Lane didn't want to keep him. "Look, I'm getting the stink eye from my beautiful wife. I need to go."

"Have a good night." The phone went dead, and Lane eased back in the couch. It wouldn't be long until he knew who the girl was.

It had been an eventful night, to say the least, and he was excited. He went to Nona's desk to get the laptop and turn it on. He wanted to check his email and wait on for the image.

"I'll see much better on this," he said to himself, bringing the thing to life. He was going to keep Nona's computer, not wanting it to get into anyone else's hands. She had lots of her personal photos on the damned thing, including nudes and lots of their flirty emails. Things Aunt Mary wouldn't want to see.

He was online for an hour before he knew it, and suddenly, he heard another noise in the house.

"What the fuck?" He turned his head and looked toward the bedroom. "It's just your imagination. Quit fucking with me, Ghost of Nona. It's not funny." He gave a little chuckle and then looked back at the screen in time to see a notification. "Yes!"

The email was in, so he quickly went to open it and download the photo. As he waited, he thought he saw something move in front of him. There was movement in the window, but that didn't make sense. Each window had blinds inside the glass, and that meant he'd seen a reflection.

From inside.

Another sound came from behind him, and then the computer screen changed to reveal the photo. He was torn as to where to look, but another glare off the computer screen told him that whatever he had heard was real and right behind him.

The knife went into his neck as the girl's face appeared on his screen. Lane froze with shock. As he slumped forward, the reflection of the woman behind him superimposed itself over the photo of her younger self.

She was the last thing he'd ever see.

CHAPTER 19

DAREK

Darek couldn't wait to get to work to see Lizzy, but as usual, because of her long hours, she was in a terrible mood.

"Here," she said, pushing a folder at him as she hurried past his desk and dropped her bag in her chair. She didn't miss a beat as she went to the coffee bar across the room to pour herself a cup.

"Good morning to you too," he said, opening the folder. "You should make that one black, like your mood." The hard look she had on her face was enough to tell him that she had a long night.

"I worked on those damn reports until three-thirty," she said. "The last time I looked at the clock before I fell asleep, it was nearly four. So, forgive me if I'm a bit grouchy."

"Why did it take you so long?" he asked.

"I wanted to make sure I covered all the bases, and then I had to do this." She walked over with her coffee and put it on the desk. After digging in her bag, she pulled out another paper. This one had Lane's statement about Otis Gough, a word for word account of the false story.

"I thought we weren't going to reveal that yet." He looked over his shoulder. "We were supposed to be biding time until we found Mia."

"Pardon my French, but screw that. I don't want to wait to go to

112

him with this. We need to get it out in the open, shake him up a bit. Then maybe he'll spill his guts about where Mia is."

"I'm not going to agree with you." He was so close to having everything, including his new job at the FBI, and he wasn't going to rock the boat and ruin things now. Max was just waiting to blab to Lizzy and anyone else who would listen, and the only reason he hadn't was to keep himself safe. As soon as he felt threatened, he was going to talk, and when he did, it would all be over.

"I can't keep this stuff from Reed forever." She downed her coffee and then dropped the empty cup in the trash. "I'm going to the little girl's room, and when I get back, you and I are going to have to find a way to see eye to eye."

As soon as she was gone, he pulled out his phone and tried to call Lane. He didn't answer, but it was probably a good thing because Lizzy was back before he knew it. "Who are you calling now?" she asked. "We have to get down to the interrogation room, Darek."

"Wait," he said. He put his phone in his pocket, and his heart raced as Lizzy got her desk phone and called down the hall to the guards.

"Could you have Maxwell Smith ready in room four in ten minutes, please?" She hung up the phone and spun around to face Darek.

"Are you serious? I think you should go home and lie down. You're clearly delusional. We talked about this. You said we'd wait until the time was right. We still have a missing girl out there, and I want to find her. You start in with him about his father, and he's going to flip out. He's going to clam up, and we're going to get zip!"

"Newsflash, Darek. We're already getting zip. I thought a lot about it last night. It's not getting us anywhere. It's time!"

Normally he'd agree with her, but he was supposed to be buying Bay time. With Lila in the hospital, Bay's focus had gone from avenging Mia to taking care of his wife and kid. Darek couldn't blame him, and while he'd been an asshole to him, he didn't wish anything bad on him, especially going to prison when he should be welcoming his child. Darek had a lot to lose too, and with one wrong move, Max would make it all go away.

"I agree to talk to him, but let's keep that in our pocket until the right time." He felt the pit of his gut turning inside out. Bile was creeping up the back of his throat, and he couldn't see any way around giving Lizzy her way. "Let's see what we can get and use that as a last resort. Please? Before we throw a wrench in everything, and he wants to talk to the press." He hated to beg her, but she rolled her eyes and reluctantly agreed.

Lizzy was frazzled, and the wild look in his eyes told him that she wasn't thinking rationally anyway. "Fine. Whatever. I'll go along with that. But if he doesn't want to talk, I'm going to have to tell him. The man thinks his father was innocent. He did all of this because he was thumbing his nose at the system. He should know what he's done. That what he did to avenge her was done for nothing! I say we wipe the smile off his smug face." She looked pissed off, and Darek understood why. She'd had faith that Otis Gough was innocent, but that wasn't the case. He had made her look like a fool.

He got up and walked over to take her into his arms. "Hey, I know you're upset. Let's not go in there guns blazing, baby."

"Get off of me," she said, pushing him away. "You're going to get us in trouble."

Darek held up his hands and backed away.

"Shit," said Lizzy. "I'm sorry, Darek."

He had rarely heard her use swear words, but when he did, he knew she was running on empty. "You should really get some rest. Call them and tell them never mind. We can go tomorrow. I think it's best."

"No, we'll go. I'm going to have another cup of coffee, and I'll be fine." She took a deep breath and scrubbed her face with her palms. "I'm sorry." She reached out and hugged him. "I know better than to let this job get to me." She quickly turned him loose and then closed her eyes to take a deep breath. "Let's go. I want to get this over with."

"It's taking a toll on all of us. It's okay to be upset about Max."

"You're not," she said. "Yet, I'm a mess. And not just about Max, but Gough. What the hell was I thinking, buying into that man's story when someone as nice as Lane was abused by him?"

Darek couldn't believe how she had taken to Lane's story, but he was the perfect person to deliver the lie. His nerves had played into the realism of his lie, and the fact that he was an all-around good guy. "Lots of people believed him."

She nodded and went to the door. Darek followed, wishing he could get out of it, but there was no way he was going to let her go alone. If Max said anything, he had to be there to dispute it. Which he would. They were more likely to take the word of two men, both upstanding members of the law enforcement community, than a man who had lied about who he was and used the badge to commit horrible crimes.

After going down to the unit where Max was being held, Darek tried not to show his emotions as they walked down the hall to the interrogation room. Lizzy had asked for room four, and Darek wondered if that was because it didn't have any recording devices, except their own.

Max waited with a blank look on his face. When Lizzy walked in ahead of Darek, Max smiled and blew her a kiss. "You miss me, sweetheart?"

"That hasn't worked for you yet," said Lizzy. "Maybe you should give up."

"No, way. I know that deep down, you want me." He chuckled, and Lizzy took a seat across from him.

"Come on, Darek. Sit down. We can arm wrestle for her." He looked down at his cuffs. "Well, shit, I'll have to take a raincheck on that one."

"I'm glad you're in a talkative mood," Darek said. "Maybe you want to tell us about Mia."

Max shrugged. "She's a tiny little thing. Fucking her made me feel kind of dirty, but knowing she was of age, I did it anyway."

"Stop it," Lizzy said. Then her phone rang, and she got up and stepped away, leaving Darek and Max alone.

"She figured you out yet?" Max asked.

"Why don't you just tell us where Mia is? It's gone on long enough. We know she's dead."

"Well, I didn't kill her." Max put his hands on the table and leaned in closer. "I fucked her good, but she was alive when I left her. I promise. I swear it on my badge." He gave a huge grin.

"Yeah, that doesn't mean much. And before you think you'll get away with anything, you'll still be responsible for her life."

"Do you have any proof that it was me? You know, solid evidence?"

"You said you took her, you said you fucked her, which I'm sure you did again, but the medical examiners can tell us that."

"You're so sure she's dead?" Max asked. "It's sad really. I wondered how many days it would take for you to give up on that poor girl. Less than a week." He shook his head and laughed. "How's her family taking it?"

Darek didn't want to go into it with him. Max didn't need the satisfaction of knowing he was responsible for Lila being in the hospital. Knowing Bay's child was in danger just might make him keep the secret of Mia's location to himself even longer.

He looked over his shoulder, wondering where Lizzy had gone. When she returned, she had a confused look on her face. "We're done here," she said, which shocked Darek. She hadn't even gotten to talk to Max. "We'll talk later."

The guards came in, and Max glared at them. "What the fuck is the problem? I wanted to have a little chit-chat."

"Not now," said Lizzy. "Later." When he was finally gone, she grabbed Darek's arm.

He was so relieved that they weren't going to talk to Max, he didn't even ask what was going on. "Well, that's that," he said.

"I just got a strange call. They gave me this address, and then they hung up." She showed him the paper she'd written it on. "That's the storage units across town."

They weren't Benny's, but they were in the same area. "Shit. This could be where she is."

"Go ahead and call Bay," said Lizzy. "We'll go and check it out before we alert anyone else. It could just be a false alarm. Make sure you tell him that. I don't want him to come if he's going to be all pissed off at a dead end." She had seen Bay's temper before.

"Okay, I'll let him know." Darek breathed a sigh of relief and prayed that this would be Mia. Knowing Max had taken her so many days earlier, there was a good chance this was a body recovery, even though he had said otherwise.

Darek took out his phone and dialed Bay's number. He knew there was no way the man wasn't going to want to come along for the ride.

CHAPTER 20

BAY

As the morning came, Lila continued to sleep, and Rose Marie sat quietly by the window reading a book. Everything had been eerily quiet since coming home from the hospital, and he was thankful they had gotten her settled in her bed.

Bay stood at the window, sipping his morning coffee and quietly looking out across the lawn.

Suddenly, Rose Marie sat forward. "Bay," she said, putting the book in her lap.

Before he could ask what was wrong, his phone rang. "It's Darek," he said. "Give me a minute?" She nodded and had a hopeless look as he answered the phone. "Hello?"

"Hey, we might have a lead on Mia," Darek said. "An anonymous tip came in. Lizzy and I don't even know if it's her, but we're going to check it out before alerting anyone else. Lizzy thought you might want to know.

"I want to go with you." He could see Rose Marie stand to her feet in his peripheral.

"Lizzy thought you might want to, but look, you can't flip out on us if it turns out to be nothing. So, if you're going to have an attitude, just stay put."

"You're the one who goes apeshit and throws people against walls," Bay said.

"Yeah, well, don't make me do it again."

Bay rolled his eyes and let the comment slide. "Give me the address. I'll meet you there." He tried to keep his voice low because of Lila's rest, but his temper was making it difficult.

"Fine, but you're closer, so you need to promise you won't go in ahead of me. I don't want anything to fuck up our investigation. We're looking at this as a recovery, not a rescue."

"I hear you loud and clear." He didn't think Mia had made it this long, either. Not with Max behind bars. She'd most likely died a week ago. He couldn't bear to think of the condition she'd be in. Cremation was the only option for his angel. He hung up the phone, and Rose Marie followed him as he walked out of the room.

"Don't tell her where I went if she wakes up," Bay told Rose Marie. "But I think we have a lead, and I'm going to go along with the detectives." Even though Lizzy was going to be with him, he still wanted to go for Mia's sake. He owed her that much.

"I'll take care of her, Bay." Her eyes were full of worry. "But I need to tell you. I don't like this, Bay. Something bad is going to happen. I saw something. It was unclear. Fast movement and then a dreadful feeling. I can't place what it is. But I have the worst feeling in my gut." She held her middle just below her breasts. "Be careful, son."

Rose Marie looked a bit ashen, and Bay feared for her health. "Are you okay?"

"I'll be fine. I'm more worried about you going off like this. Promise me you'll take care."

"I will," he said.

Her hard stare penetrated him. "Don't do anything in haste, Bay." With that, she gave him a pat on the back and walked back into the room with Lila. She had stayed by her and the baby's side all night and would likely be there when the baby came.

"Yes, ma'am," he said to himself. She worried him when she became so troubled, but he had no way of knowing what her vision had meant. She just knew things. Sometimes, it was more specific than others, but Bay knew her gifts were special.

He headed out, and when he got in his car, he looked at his phone for the address Darek sent him. The place was across town, but Bay would still make it there a few minutes before the cops, even though he'd taken time for Rose Marie's warning. And putting his pedal down just might get him there quicker.

Bay got hung up behind an overturned car on the expressway, so when he got to the storage place, he was actually a few minutes behind the detectives. They were about to head in without him when he pulled up.

"What kept you?" asked Darek as Bay got out of the car. Lizzy was standing near the front of her car, and she had a smug look on her face. Bay knew there was no love lost between them, but he'd never liked her type.

"Traffic," Bay said. "Overturned car. I'm guessing you heard the call out?"

Darek nodded. "I did. Just didn't think it was on your way. Was it bad?"

"I didn't care to look. Glad I got here when I did, though." He gave Lizzy a pointed look. "Agent McNamara, thank you for the invite. Can we get this rolling? I have a distraught wife at home, and I'd like to give her a bit of closure when she wakes up."

"Sure thing," Lizzy said. "I hope she's okay. Darek had just told me she had to be rushed to the hospital."

"Yes," he answered as they walked toward the door of the storage unit. "She and the baby are perfect. Just needed some rest."

"It must be horrible, worrying about someone you love in such a delicate state. Let's hope that everything works out for your family." She seemed sincere enough, but Bay didn't like her tone very much. It was somewhere between sympathy and pity. He had no use for either.

"I'm sure they'll appreciate your concern," he said.

The door to the unit opened up. It was much like the unit at Benny's, only it didn't smell of rotting blood and it was also three times bigger. Lights dimly lit their path. Boxes were stacked everywhere, and this time, it looked like some kind of fixtures and plumbing parts.

"Was this a contractor's unit?" asked Lizzy.

"At some point in time," said Bay. "Looks like this place hasn't been used in a while, though. Look at the dust and the cobwebs."

Suddenly, a noise stopped them in their tracks. It was a tiny squeal that almost sounded like a mouse.

"Shit, there's rats in here," said Darek.

"Let's keep quiet, and keep moving," Lizzy said. "We might hear it again."

As they moved on, the sound of something sliding across the floor stopped them again. Lizzy held her hand up for them to stop walking, and they all listened as the sound continued and stopped. She took her gun out of its holster, and Darek, who had already pulled his, readied his weapon to continue.

Bay strained his ears, and when he heard the sound again, it was all too familiar. "Mia. That's Mia."

He started to move forward, but Lizzy put a hand on his shoulder, and Darek held him back.

"It's probably just a rat," said Lizzy.

"Can we step it up?" Bay asked. "I'm not moving at a goddamned snail's pace here. I'm almost certain that's a person I hear. If anyone knows Mia's squeals, it's me."

Darek shook his head. "I'd like to believe that too, and I know how much imagination can play tricks when we really want something to be true."

That not only insulted Bay, but it had his temper flaring. "To hell with both of you." He pushed Lizzy out of the way and started forward, but Darek stopped him.

"She's right. We're going, but we're not going to trample evidence *if* she's in there. Look. She's been here a while, Bay, if she is. Let me go first. You don't want to see her like that. Especially if there are rats."

Bay realized what he was hearing could be rats fighting over her flesh. "Fine."

They still had a ways to go to get to the back, but they pushed on through the rows of boxes until Bay heard another sound, and he moved a little faster.

Finally, they came around a corner where the overhead light was brighter. "There." Lizzy pointed ahead, and they moved forward, with her just steps ahead of Bay and Darek on their tail. "Something is—"

Lizzy's words were drowned out by a loud squealing sound, and when Bay looked up, he saw Mia's eyes, wide and pleading.

"Mia!" He started forward, closing the distance to get to her, but Lizzy put a hand on his shoulder.

"Stop, she's alive, and we're going to get her out of here, but I need you to listen to me. This is a crime scene. Proceed with care."

Bay turned to look at his Mia. She squealed louder, the ball gag in her mouth making it impossible for her to speak. She was tied face-down on a board, her body stripped naked, blood coating her like a second skin. How she was alive was anyone's guess. But it meant that Max had never been in on this alone.

"Fuck you and your crime scene!" He hurried over, and as he approached, Mia's sounds became more pleading.

"Don't worry, Mia. I've got you." He had to get the gag off her, but as he walked over to undo the clip, he saw that she was carved up. "I'm going to kill that asshole. You mark my words. I'll cut his fucking heart out and eat it!"

As the gag's clasp popped open, Mia's eyes filled with horror, and four long blades pierced her middle, protruding through her back.

"No!" said Bay, realizing what had happened. He backed away as the life drained from his little girl, his most prized pet, his Mia.

"Fucking hell," said Darek, who shot forward, grabbing Bay and pulling him away. "There could be more. This whole place could be one big trap."

For the first time in his life, Bay was frozen still. He couldn't comprehend what had happened, and he couldn't stop thinking how close he'd been to having her back. Max had not taken her twice, but three times.

And he'd made the last one count.

Lizzy stepped over and took her pulse. "She's gone. Darek, call the units. She's got some serious wounds." She turned to Bay. "Look at her back, Mr. Collins."

Bay stepped around to where he could see the damage that had been done to Mia's back. Not only had she been held captive, but she'd been stripped naked and tied to a board that had been specially designed to pierce every fatal target possible, including her heart. The blades had been so long that they had pierced through her back and through the Zodiac wheel that had been crudely carved into her back. She looked just like Emily Johnson, except for one detail, which Lizzy pointed out.

"They're all the same sign," she said. "My guess would be Scorpio." She turned to Bay, placing her hand on his left shoulder, right over the place where Bay had been branded with the same sign years ago. "I'm guessing that's you?"

There wasn't any denying his involvement now. He could rat Darek out to his girl and blow up the entire fucking world, but Bay did something he never thought he could. He reached up and undid the top two buttons on his shirt and then pulled his collar to the side. "Yeah, the asshole molested me too."

He hoped that with him and Lane both telling the same story, it would be a much stronger case, and because of his status in the community, he hoped he could keep the press out of it.

"I'm going to have a lot of questions," said Lizzy. She reached over and closed Mia's eyes.

"I've got the answers." He didn't know what it was going to mean for his life and his reputation, but as long as it could buy his freedom, that was all that mattered.

He turned to Darek. "I want to see that asshole. Make it happen." He'd watched the life drain out from Mia's eyes, and he'd do the same to Max. It was just like Rose Marie had said. Something quick and then pain. "He set this up. He fixed it so I'd be the one to kill her."

"He had no way of knowing you'd be here." Darek slumped as he released a long breath. "Max had help for this."

Bay gave him a knowing look. "Yeah, he did." He didn't need to say her name. Darek knew who Bay thought it was.

CHAPTER 21

DAREK

After calling in the death and having the place combed for other traps, which came back clear, Darek led Lizzy and Bay back into the building. Mia was still strapped to the board, and her photo was being taken.

Bay grimaced. "She'd hate that," he said as the camera flashed. "She always wanted to be camera ready. She used to want to be a model, you know? But she was so petite, and she had too much pride for catalog work. She wanted to be on the runway. That's when she decided she'd just make the clothes and bags. She really could have made it."

"She was a good girl," said Darek. It was the most he'd heard Bay say nice about anyone in a long time. "I'm so sorry for how it went down. I also know what you're thinking, and I'm not getting into it with you over Raven, but I also can't let you go down to the station until you've calmed down. I'll see about arranging something in a few days."

Bay watched as Lizzy walked over to talk to the photographer, pointing out things she wanted catalogued.

"This shit was designed to hurt me when I found it," Bay said.

"The killer couldn't have known you'd be here," Darek said. "That's totally against protocol."

Bay shook his head. "Then maybe you were supposed to kill her. Either way, Max didn't go through the trouble of all of this, keeping his fucking mouth shut and waiting like a fiend until we stumbled on Mia. Someone else orchestrated this shit."

"On that, we agree," said Darek.

Bay nodded. "That anonymous tip? Did Lizzy say who it came from? Male or female?"

"No," Darek said. "We were down in the interrogation room, about to talk to Max when it all went down. Someone called, but I never heard the conversation."

"My money is on female," Bay said.

"Come on, man. Let's not do this now." He glanced at Bay with weary eyes. "We need to keep it together. Shit's about to get ugly. I tell you, if Lizzy ever pops this on him, he's going to blow."

Bay nodded. "I'll call Lane and warn him. And tell him about Mia." He let out a long breath. "Christ, I've got to go home and tell Lila. When she asks how it happened, how am I going to tell her this shit? That it was ultimately my fault?"

"It isn't your fault. It was set up to make you feel like that, but Max did this."

"Him and someone else," Bay said.

Lizzy walked over. "The CSI guys are here, getting photos and fingerprints. I hope that whoever did this for Max was sloppy. Maybe we'll find some DNA. It looked as if she had some vaginal bleeding. I'm not sure if that's from her cycle or if she was assaulted."

Darek wanted to tell Bay that if she was raped by a man, it couldn't have been Raven involved. With Lizzy around, he had to hold that back. "Maybe it was his brother, Otis Jr. He could have been in on this with his brother all along."

Bay all but spat. "You'd like that to be true, wouldn't you? I'm pretty sure that's Mia's period. The assholes gave her no fucking dignity. I guess I can be glad she wasn't pregnant."

"We'll call you when those things come out," Lizzy said. "If Mia was pregnant, the blood could be a miscarriage from the stress."

Bay's nostrils flared. "Thanks," he said through gritted teeth. "Isn't she just a shining example of empathy?"

Lizzy walked back over to the body, giving Darek a regretful look.

"She's just in her work headspace," Darek said, feeling the need to defend her. "She's like a whole different person when she's focused on work."

"Who gives a shit?" Bay asked. "I want Max. I'm going to check with my feelers, see if they found a way to get to him."

"Be careful," said Darek under his breath.

"I'm going to make sure that someone pays for this. Soon."

"Don't do anything stupid." He wondered if Bay would try to go after Raven, but he realized Bay would probably leave her alone, knowing she was still in Nashville. Darek considered warning Bay against it, but he didn't want to put any ideas in Bay's head.

Lizzy walked back over. "Before we move her, would you like a moment with her?"

Bay's chest swelled with a deep breath, but it didn't do anything to cleanse the stormy expression from his face. He walked over and brushed her hair back from her face. Tears were still wet on her cheeks. Bay must have seen them too because he brushed them away.

"I'm sorry, Mia," he whispered. Darek noticed he didn't shed a tear of his own, but he had never seen Bay look so pale before, like a ghost of himself.

Bay walked away without another word and left the building.

Lizzy joined Darek's side. "I can't believe he didn't tell us about his involvement. To think the victims of Gough's crimes were right in front of us the whole time, along with the killer? I don't know about you, but I'm getting tired of the surprises."

Darek shook his head. "He's a victim. He's ashamed." He still couldn't believe that Bay had told Lizzy he'd been molested, too. "I think these men are concerned about their privacy. Both have a lot to lose. We need to make sure we keep this under wraps until necessary."

"I still think we have to nail Max's balls to the wall," Lizzy said.

"And find out who helped him. He didn't have Mia strapped up like this all on his own. This took skill and planning. They've been coming here to take care of her, without a doubt. So, we need to see if there are any security cameras around this area. Something that might show us who has been coming and going."

Darek just hoped that it wouldn't show Raven. He knew in his heart it was a stupid theory, but his brain couldn't help wonder. No, someone else had to be close to this case, and he was willing to bet it was Otis Jr. or whoever Emily's sister turned out to be. *Anyone but Raven.*

And even though he was ticked off at Bay, he knew he shouldn't be alone. Someone needed to watch him. Darek dialed Lane's number, hoping he'd be up for the task, but got no answer.

CHAPTER 22

BAY

After what happened, Bay couldn't face Lila to tell her. He feared too much for his child, more than for his stubborn wife. She already resented him for having a boy like he wanted, and not the daughter she wanted to turn into her little clone.

Instead, he wanted to get away by himself and thought his crow's nest at Taunt was the perfect place to be alone.

Mia had hated it there in the end, but he still remembered the first day he'd brought her up there when she wasn't quite legal. He had respected her until she was, but her curiosity had gotten the better of them both, and he wanted to sneak her in and let her see what kind of life he had to offer her. She was hooked from the very first night, and he'd left her to be alone with herself to get the full effect.

She had always been so curious, and when she confessed that she'd been watching him and Lila have sex, he knew she was going to be interesting.

"You are so hot," she'd said. "I can't wait until I can have you. All Lila does is lie there." Which wasn't entirely true. "You need someone who bites back."

So, just like she was still there with him, he could people watch from his observation deck and hopefully drink enough to forget the sound of the blades ripping through Mia's flesh like she was nothing but a paper doll. As long as he lived, he'd never get over the sound of the metal chipping past her bones, the gurgle in her throat, and the way her eyes stilled. The expression on her face had faded as the muscles stopped doing their job. She had slipped away right before his eyes.

He had never wondered what was on the other side, but he hoped that wherever Mia was, it was pink.

After stopping off for one of his favorite vodkas—one so expensive he didn't bother keeping it stocked for the club patrons—he turned off the highway, onto the side street where he could easily get to the back lot. He pulled his car back there to use his private entrance, where his security and staff parked, and he noticed that there was already a nice little crowd forming at the front door. The early night crowd was tame compared to the late-night arrivers, but at least they weren't as worried about being discreet, which fascinated him even more.

As he got out of his car, already sipping his poison straight from the bottle, he saw someone walking across the lot.

"You sneaky bitch," he said.

He walked across the lot and into the back door, where he stepped inside and saw Raven speaking with the security guard.

"I'm only here to see Eve," she said in a defensive tone. "She told me to use the back door. I'm not paying you a cover charge so you can go and snort it up your fat nose."

Bay was amused at how she handled his guard, and everything she'd said about him was true. "It's okay," said Bay. "I'll take it from here."

Raven's back stiffened before she spun around. "Great," she muttered.

"Funny to see you here," he said.

"Is it? I used to practically live here. Shouldn't be too much of a shock." She crossed her arms, clutching the shopping bag full of what looked like clothes from Bay's perspective.

"And you obviously think that gives you backdoor privileges?" Bay felt a surge of victory. Seeing Raven in New York was all the proof he needed. She'd been the one to help Max, and he was going to prove it. But first, he was going to have a little fun.

Raven scowled at him. "I'm only here because I'm selling Eve some of my things."

"You need money? I thought that last lover of yours left you well off. What happened? Did Nate take you out of the will?"

"No, it's not that. It's just, I'm going to lead a much tamer life in Nashville, so I don't exactly have any use for hooker boots and leather panties." She gave a shrug, and Bay thought of how good she would look in a pair of leather panties and nothing else.

And then he imagined her on fire, wondering how she would scream.

He had to ask. "So why come back to New York? Darek made it sound like you were gone for good."

The poor bastard was going to be heartbroken when he found out that she was involved. Darek had fallen for the woman, and no matter what happened to him and his partner, he would always love her. Some things weren't easy to let go. Like Mia.

Raven frowned. "Not that it's any of your business, but Noah's here. I came back for him. Once he's released, we're moving to Nashville for good. I've got all the arrangements in order for the bed and breakfast, so if you're ever in Nashville, *don't* look me up."

She was sticking to her story, but Bay wasn't buying it. She had probably been in New York the whole time. She thought she'd get in and out of Taunt without Bay noticing, since he didn't usually go there so early.

"How long have you been back in the city?" he asked.

"Just landed a few hours ago. I had all of this shit in my luggage for Eve, and I'm making room for Noah's things when I go back home."

Bay winked at her. "Don't worry. I won't tell Darek I saw you. You know, Mia always wanted to go to Nashville." She hadn't really. He just wanted to read Raven's expression.

Raven narrowed her eyes. "Did she?" She showed no emotion

either way as Bay carefully watched her eyes. "You should bring her sometime." She turned and started to walk away, but Bay wasn't going to have this whore turning her back on him.

He put his bottle on the floor and hurried to grab her arm. "Little late for that, don't you think?"

"I beg your pardon?" She gave him another hard stare, and Bay could tell she was dying to get away from him.

"Never mind," Bay said. "How about you come up to the office and wait for Eve with me? You know, out of all the Zodiacs, I've never had the pleasure of your company. Yet you frequented my club more than anyone else. I think I'm the only Zodiac you know that you haven't had a taste of. We should remedy that, don't you think?"

He knew she'd never go along with it, and while he'd never forced his cock on anyone else, he wanted to shake her up with the suggestion.

She jerked herself away. "I think I should find Eve myself." She held the bag closer to her side, as if for protection.

Bay grabbed her and pulled her back to him. "I think you need a lesson in control." As she struggled, Bay pushed open the downstairs storage room and crowded her inside. "You like others to be in control, don't you? I bet you'd love a good lesson."

"You're out of your mind." Her jaw was so tight, he could see the muscles twitch. "Get the fuck off me, Bay. I'm not here for that, and I'd *never* be with you."

"Why is that? Have you heard what a reprehensible bastard I am? Do you know my demons?"

"Get off me," she growled. "Before you see *my* demons."

Bay reached down and cupped her mound. "That's the thanks I get for all of those hot nights you spent in ecstasy in my house? Unacceptable. Besides, our demons want to play together."

"Eve will be coming soon," she said with a hard tone. Her eyes were as wild as a cornered cat's. "Remove your hand, Bay."

Bay smirked. "Come on. Let me inside you, Raven. Be a good girl for me. Turn around and touch your toes. I promise to fuck you good and hard, just like you like it. We can talk about our secrets. I know you have secrets, Raven. A dark-haired, mysterious woman like yourself. And you know I do too. My secrets interest you a lot, don't they? You know you wanted to hear the truth; the whole story. I can tell you everything." With each word, he pressed harder, rubbing between her legs. "I bet you're wet for me already."

Raven narrowed her eyes, and he heard the bag she held rustling. Then she held something cool to his neck. "Let me go, or we'll see how long it takes my dull blade to cut you."

Bay removed his hands and stepped back. "Well now, Ms. Bishop. Interesting choice of weapon. Do you always carry knives with you?"

The old dagger was long enough to do some serious damage to bone and organs.

"Only when I fear running into assholes like you," she said. "I'm not one of your fucking victims, Bay. I'm not some little girl you can manipulate and take advantage of."

"Don't sell yourself short, lover. Or me. I'm full of surprises, as you'll soon see." He wasn't talking about sex. He was going to shock the hell out of her when Max died in jail. What would she do with herself then? Sooner or later, he'd have them both on their backs.

Raven let out a nervous sort of laugh. "You really *do* think you're some kind of fucking god, don't you? But I know you better. I know you're nothing but a regular piece of shit like everyone else. I wish that bullet back in New Orleans would have done you in." She met his eyes while pointing the blade at his face. "If you ever put a hand on me again, I'll cut you so deep, your children will feel it."

She had a glazed-over look in her eyes, and she quickly pushed him aside and marched out into the hall. Something in her cold eyes gave Bay chills.

Bay's reaction was a shock. Somehow, she had managed to make his cock hard. "Impressive." He suddenly saw what all of those others saw in her, that special fire of passion. He also saw a stone-cold killer.

Footsteps sounded behind him. "Where did she run off to?" asked Eve, standing just outside the supply room. She seemed lost as a goose. "I was going to buy some of her things. It's hard to find anyone the same size boot like me."

Bay looked down where Raven had left the bag of clothes and picked them up. "Here, she left these. She said to pick what you like, and you can pay her later."

She wasn't the only one. Bay was going to pay back that sneaky bitch, too.

CHAPTER 23

DAREK

Because of the shitshow that Mia's rescue had turned into, Darek had been at the scene until late in the night. Waking to a new day, he wondered how long his own name could be kept out of the mix. He needed to think of an excuse that could get him out of hot water with Lizzy if it all went south. She'd either believe him, or she wouldn't.

They still had to find Max's accomplice. As soon as he got to the station, Darek had Otis Jr. dragged in. Lizzy busied herself down at Dr. Cobb's office.

Now, Darek headed down to the interrogation room, where Otis was waiting for him. When Darek joined him, Otis had a grim look on his face.

"How much longer am I going to have to sit here?" Otis rapped his knuckles on the table. "I haven't done anything wrong, and I don't appreciate being hauled down here this early. I have a family, kids to get to school, and work."

"It says here you're unemployed," said Darek.

"Looking for work. Whatever. You're wasting my valuable time."

Darek sat at the table across from him. "Being unemployed must give you time to do lots of things. Like take up new hobbies. Do you have any hobbies?"

"I like to work on my bike," Otis said, shrugging.

"You're good with machines?" The contraption that had killed Mia must have been a serious project. A little mechanical knowhow would go a long way. Darek leaned in closer. "Do you know who I am?"

Otis frowned. "No fucking clue, man. When are you going to get me out of here? Just because my brother is a fuck up doesn't mean I am."

"Your brother was locked up when the last crime was committed," Darek said.

"Is this about that missing girl?" Otis asked. Darek wondered if he was going to rat Bay and Lane out. "I called that guy back and told him everything I knew. I told him all about Emily's sister and cooperated. He can vouch for me. I have nothing to hide."

"You seem exceptionally nervous for a man who is innocent," said Darek. So far, the guy hadn't let on that he knew Darek at all, which made Darek question his theory. Then again, Max had been a hell of a liar too.

"My father died in prison after being arrested for a crime he didn't commit. Forgive me for being a bit rattled by the idea that the same thing could happen to me."

"Why are you so sure that your father was innocent?" Darek asked.

"He said so. He said he woke up and there she was. He went over to check on her, found her dead. I had never seen my father cry until that moment. And the zodiac, he didn't even believe in that shit."

"He had a zodiac tattoo," Darek said.

Otis shook his head. "No, that was something he got in the fucking military. He didn't even know what it was. One of his buddies had it on his arm. When he died, he got the tattoo in remembrance of his friend. I think it was like Capricorn or something. I don't even know. My dad used to say that fortune-telling stuff was bullshit."

Darek believed him. He almost certainly didn't have anything to do with Mia's death. Still, Darek needed to keep pressing to be sure. "The missing girl was kept hidden for nearly a week. We could tell that she was fed, given water, and allowed to use the bathroom, but she was strapped to a device that stabbed her while we were trying to free her."

"Well, there you go," Otis said. "My brother was locked up. He couldn't have been involved, right?"

Darek looked at the man. He looked so much like Max it was crazy. "Your brother had been stabbing his victims and leaving marks of the zodiac, just like Emily Johnson. This poor little girl was strapped naked to a board and carved up like a slab of meat. Then just when she thought she'd have a chance at being saved, she was killed."

Darek had a feeling Mia knew about the trigger all along, and that was why she started squealing, to try and warn them. If she hadn't had the ball gag in her mouth, she could have said something, and they could have disarmed the device. Whoever had set it up, it was just like Bay said. They had hoped either he or Darek would find her and trigger the knives. If it wasn't one of them, the device was still a great way to ensure she didn't rat out whoever her kidnapper was.

Tears came to his eyes. "Dear God, he's an animal. What happened to him? He used to be a decent guy. The trial? What happened to our old man? It made him turn sour. He's evil. I have a little girl myself. I can't even fathom." He squeezed his eyes shut tightly. "I'd kill the son of a bitch. He should be locked away forever."

"I agree with you, and with any luck, he will," Darek said. "But we're still looking for whoever helped him. Do you have any ideas?"

Otis nodded. "I told Lane Simon about a girlfriend my brother had. He was head over heels for her. They had some crazy sex shit going on. I'm not into all of that weird shit."

"I feel ya," said Darek. He wanted to tell him not to knock it until he tried it, but thinking of that only made him think of Raven. "What was the girlfriend's name?"

"I really never knew it. Like I told the others, I might know her if I saw her."

Darek took out the composite of Raven that had been tucked into the case file. "Could this be her?" He held his breath as the man studied the photo.

Otis let out a long breath. "I don't know. I hate to say it and put some innocent person in trouble, but it *could* be her. I mean, she had dark hair, petite features. She was pretty, but this drawing doesn't really do her justice."

Darek took the photo back and put it in the folder. "So, you're not sure?"

"No, I'm not," Otis said. "Sorry. Maybe if I saw a photograph. My brother might have one of them somewhere. Have you checked his house?"

"A couple of times, but we might look again. I'd advise you to stay away from there. The place is locked up tight."

"No problem there," Otis said. "I haven't talked to Max in over a year."

"Thank you for coming in," said Darek. "I'll be in touch." With that, Darek got up and walked to the door.

"Good luck, Detective."

Darek went down the hall, cursing under his breath. That was a dead end.

His phone rang about the time he got to his office to type up a report for his personal use, and seeing it was Bay, he let out a sigh and answered. "Hey, how are you holding up?"

"I'm just fucking dandy. And you'll never believe who I saw last night, right there at the sex club just like she always was."

Darek's blood pumped faster. "Raven is in Nashville."

"Is she? Because if that's true, her fucking doppelganger is in town. I spoke with her, though, so I'm pretty sure she wasn't a figment of my imagination."

"That doesn't mean she's involved," Darek said.

"It's Zodiac business. She's always fucking involved, and you know it. Somehow, someway, Raven's in the goddamned middle. And let me just warn you now, Darek. If I find out that cunt had anything to do with Mia's murder, I'm going to slice her open and watch her slowly bleed out, and I just might make you watch."

"You're getting pretty bold, Bay. Do you know that?" He knew Bay was capable of all sorts of brutality. The man was crazy and had no regard for human life himself. "If you touch one fucking hair on her head, I swear to God."

"You better check your girl, then," Bay said. "I'd make damned sure, Darek."

His heart was beating so fast, it was all he could hear. Bay's voice had taken on the sound of a hollow tube. He hung up the phone and forced himself to breathe.

Lizzy still hadn't gotten back. Even so, he got up and went to the bathroom, where he made sure no one was around when he locked the outside door. When he knew he was alone, he dialed Raven's number.

"Darek?" she answered.

"What the fuck are you doing in town?" he asked.

"Excuse me? I don't have to tell you my every move, Darek. I'm not your girlfriend, remember?"

"How long have you been here?"

"A few days," she said. "Why does it matter?"

"Someone killed Mia, is why. They took her and killed her in the worst fucking way, and I don't want that to be you. I want you to be safe, okay? Is that too much to fucking ask of you?"

Her tone hardened. "Jesus. Mia? Shit. That's why Bay was acting so fucking weird."

"Well, he's got it in his head that you're somehow involved," Darek said.

"He's sick in the head. He was drinking, and well, it's embarrassing, but he tried to assault me."

Darek swallowed hard. "Assault?"

"He grabbed me between my legs and came onto me in the grossest, most foul way."

Darek's blood boiled. "Are you shitting me? He tried to fuck you?"

"Yeah. I got out of there as soon as I could."

"I'm going to break his fucking neck," said Darek. He was going to drive right over and choke the fucker out. "I'll handle him."

"Darek, stop. I'm not yours to worry about. I'm not yours to protect. And in case you've forgotten, I'm not exactly a delicate little flower who someone like Bay could leave trembling from a sexual advance."

"You're a lady, and ladies shouldn't be grabbed and molested. He's going to fucking pay for that shit. Did he say anything to you? Anything about what's going on?"

"Not about Mia. God, that's just awful. She was so young, and she really tried, you know? I felt bad for her situation, but she pulled through for Bay when it counted. I know he's hurting."

"No, that's not a fucking pass to act like a dick." Bay had done some low things, but this was the lowest.

"I know," she said. "I just don't want you to react this way."

"I know, baby. I'm sorry I called in such a shitty mood."

"Darek, you're doing it again. Look. I know you mean well, but how long are you going to call me up, worried about me? After you're married to some other woman?"

"I know. Lizzy would have a fit if she knew I called. I just couldn't help it. I didn't really think you were back."

"Sorry, but I'm not going to call you every time I'm in town, Darek. I've got to move on with my life. I know I'm the one who dicked things up, but it doesn't make it any easier to move on alone. Mixed signals do not help."

She had asked for space before, and he just kept crowding her. But in his defense, she was being accused of murder. But after talking to her, he knew she couldn't possibly have been lying to him. He would have been able to tell.

"Forgive me, again," he said. "I'll try and remember you asked for space."

"It's always good to hear from you, you know? I keep waiting for the day that you call me up and tell me you miss me. I know it's not going to happen, but a girl can dream." She let out a sigh. "Goodbye again, Darek."

He *did* miss her, but he didn't tell her. "Goodbye, Raven."

He hung up the phone and then went to the sink to wash his hands. He heard a knock at the door.

"Why is this locked?" called a familiar voice on the other side. "Someone get the janitor."

Darek unlocked the door and found Darius standing on the other side. "Sorry," he said. "I needed a phone booth."

"Oh, well next time, take it to your car. Some of us have to take a piss." He pushed past Darek and headed for the nearest urinal. Darius had been acting distant since Max's arrest, and he wasn't the only one.

Lizzy met him in the hall. "What were you doing in there?"

"Shitting," he lied.

"Gross."

He shrugged. "Tell me what you found out about Mia."

"Sure," Lizzy said. "She was well fed and hydrated, as we expected. And about six weeks pregnant. I don't think she knew about it."

"Fuck. Don't tell Bay. He'll really lose it."

"He needs the truth, and I want to talk to him anyway. We're about to bust the case wide open with this pedophile ring. Who knows there might be other victims out there, others who deserve justice." She had that cold, hard look in her eyes that she only got when she was focused on the job. "We have to get this case wrapped up."

"Give him another day. We have enough work to do without dragging him in and making it all worse. Think of his wife and baby."

"Darek, if you keep thinking of everyone but yourself, you'll never get your spot at the FBI. Sometimes, you have to do the hard thing and tell the truth. It's not always pretty, but in the end, it's the *right* thing. He should know everything, and I don't think he'd appreciate us waiting." She let out a long breath. "But since it means that much to you, I'll at least wait until they release Mia's body. That will lessen the blow, I'm sure."

CHAPTER 24

BAY

Waking up with a pounding head, Bay rolled over, hoping to find his nightstand at home. Instead, he found that he'd not only ended up back at his penthouse, but he hadn't gone there alone.

The blonde beside him had nothing on Mia. Not only was she not thin, not pretty, and not as good in bed, but her personality left a lot to be desired as well. She stirred, letting out a moan that wasn't going to tempt him in any way.

"Get the fuck up," he said, pushing at her shoulder. "It's time to go."

"Do you want to take a shower?" she asked, shielding her eyes as the morning sun shone across her pale, freckly face.

"No." His voice was firm, and in no way should it have given her a false sense of security.

"Oh, boo. I'll blow you if you want. I bet it would put you in a much better mood."

"Look, Marissa, the beer goggles are gone. You should go before I have to be rude."

Her mouth hung open like she didn't understand. "You sure seemed to like it last night." She got up with his expensive sheet wrapped around her like a toga and gathered her things. "And my name is Clarissa."

Bay reached into his wallet and threw down two twenties on the bed. "That should cover your trouble and cab fare." It was about thirty-eight dollars more than the two-dollar whore deserved, but the sooner she left, the better. She had served her purpose, which had been to get him off.

She gathered the bills and her clothes and quickly changed, leaving the sheet on the floor across the room. "You're an asshole. If I see you at the club, do me a favor and don't talk to me."

Bay didn't bother with a response. The girl wasn't one of his regulars or a valued customer, and she had no idea he was the owner. He listened to her mumble under her breath as she grabbed her bag and headed to the door.

Once she had the door open, she called back to him. "You weren't so fucking special yourself, freak." With that, she shut the door.

Bay was glad it was quiet, and he went to the bathroom for something to take for his headache. Then he texted Rose Marie to tell her he was still alive. How he'd managed to pull off a bender, bag a skank, and forget everything he needed to do was beyond him, but he needed to get on with his day. His phone rang, and he assumed it was Rose Marie, taking the text as a cue to call him. When he looked at the phone, it was a different number, one he had been waiting to see.

"Lawrence Bradford," Bay said. "I do hope you're calling me with good news."

The man spoke in a low tone. "I heard you needed a new man. Wondered if I could get in on the gig."

"I need someone to be somewhere at a certain time of night. Do you think you could make that happen?"

"That depends on the price. I've got a medical emergency and some family issues."

"Sounds like I could help," Bay said. "I'll pay you cash, and I'll throw in an extra twenty for your kid. You really should start thinking of his future." Bay needed the man to know that he was in, but also that he better not fuck him over.

"Call me when you're ready." The man hung up the phone, and Bay breathed a sigh of relief. Max would soon get his, and Bay would be nowhere around for the aftermath. He planned on taking Lila and hiding out until after the baby was born.

He decided to call Lane and tell him all about Raven and how the bitch had been in town the entire time. She had to be involved, and even though Darek had a soft spot for her, Bay was going to make sure she was taken care of, just like Max.

He dialed Lane's number and waited for him to answer. When he didn't, Bay decided he needed to go over and check in on him.

He left the penthouse and got in his car, finding the Marissa/Clarissa's panties in the front seat. He lowered the window and tossed them out. Then he raced across town to see Lane, who was most likely still asleep at Nona's or too busy moving her shit out that he didn't have time to answer.

Bay arrived after a ten-minute drive and was relieved to see Lane's car. He was looking forward to telling Lane that their troubles with Max would soon be over. The man was as good as dead. Bay just had to get his thugs on the inside to be ready to strike.

He almost expected Lane to meet him at the door, but he figured the man was doing something that kept him from it. Bay rang the bell, but Lane never answered. It wasn't until Bay looked in the window and could see the back of Lane's head that he began to be suspicious that all was not well.

He banged on the door again. "Lane?"

He banged on the door, pounding his fist harder than he wanted to. The man had to hear that.

But Lane didn't budge.

Bay looked into another window, but he couldn't see Lane from that angle. He went back to the door and looked under the mat for the key.

"Bingo," he said. "Lane!" His voice was full of excitement as he opened the door, but then, when Lane still didn't respond, he began to think that something was wrong; something terrible.

"Lane, if you're asleep sitting up, I'm going to beat you until you wake up." He walked into the room and stopped short when he saw blood dripping down the back of the couch. "Dammit."

Lane sat there with a knife wound in his neck, and he had a laptop on the coffee table in front of him. Bay walked in front of him.

Lane's eyes had been removed from their sockets and were lying bloody in the palms of his hands. "Oh shit, brother. What have they done to you?" His shirt was pulled open, exposing his brand on his shoulder, and the stab wounds were so violent, Lane looked like mincemeat.

Bay took Lane's phone and put it in his pocket. He didn't want him to be found with it. Whoever he'd spoken to last might have some clues to share. He took his own phone out, dialed nine-one-one, and reported the crime. Then he called Darek.

Darek answered his phone with a shitty tone. "What the fuck do you want?" he asked.

"Lane's dead." It had come down to the two of them, even though Max was locked up and they thought they'd had their man just two days earlier.

"Shit. What happened?" Darek's tone changed to that of concern.

"He's sitting here in Nona's house with his eyes in his lap. He also had a computer in front of him. I'm guessing he knew too much, saw something he shouldn't have. He was still on the case."

"Fuck," said Darek.

"Yeah, you can say that again. It's all one big fuck you to us. Do you still want to ignore that there is another person involved?"

"We're not ignoring it, Bay. We've had Otis in. I thought it was him, but it's not."

"No, it's not. I think you should ask your friend where she was," Bay said.

"Getting almost raped by you," Darek said. "Yeah, I know what happened with you and her. She told me how you tried to fuck her. That doesn't tell me you think she's guilty of anything, Bay."

"I do, and don't worry. I wasn't trying to fuck her as much as I was trying to rattle her."

"Oh, you did," Darek said. "Keep your fucking hands off her. And don't touch Lane, either. I'll be right there."

"Be warned. It's pretty gruesome. And as much as I hate to say it, it's so bloody that maybe you were right. Maybe Raven didn't have anything to do with it." He didn't totally believe it, but he just couldn't see a chick doing something so brutal. Carving out Lane's eyes? Whoever had done it was fucking nuts.

He hung up the phone and looked at the scene, wondering what was on the computer. The battery was dead, and Bay checked Lane's phone battery, as well as his ringtone volume, just to see if it was still working. When he was sure he had enough charge, he went to the texts and found one from Kenneth Warner. The man had most likely found something, and Bay was going to find out what.

CHAPTER 25

DAREK

Lizzy had been working day and night to find out all she could about Mia's death. Darek had been equally as busy trying to nail down evidence and keep things from imploding. So, after Bay had called about Lane's death, he went into the building and found Lizzy hurrying down the hall.

"We had a call," she said.

"Homicide, in the Belvedere area?"

"Yes, how'd you know?" Her eyes narrowed. "I just got the call. It was *just* phoned in." She didn't look pleased, and she let out a long breath.

"I got a call, too. It's Lane."

"Lane Simon?" She put a hand over her mouth and turned away, as if looking him in the eye might make it all true.

"Yeah. Bay went to check on him and found him. He says it's pretty gruesome. I'd assume he's stabbed like the rest. Bay said he had his eyes cut out."

"Dear Lord," said Lizzy. "That's new." Her face paled. "What kind of monster are we dealing with?"

"I don't know, but we need to get going." He thought of Bay being

146

there with Lane, sitting there staring at someone who couldn't stare back.

"I'll drive." She walked past him and headed to the parking lot. Darek hurried to keep up, and soon, they were on their way.

"We have to figure out who is helping Max," Darek said. "He's surely pulling strings from the inside, but who could be in on this with him? Who would have the biggest motive?"

"It's probably someone who wants revenge too," said Lizzy. She turned out onto the main road.

Darek wasn't so sure. "Or a call to loyalty. If Max has someone who loved him enough to see the whole thing play out, then it's probably safe to say he could control them without a problem from prison. Or perhaps they had something else to go by, with him locked up. A schedule? Things were pretty well-planned with Mia's death, and he obviously didn't do it alone."

"It was sadistic," she said. "Makes my stomach sick. Whoever these people are, they're the worst."

Darek wondered if that could be the point. To do something so horrible and hope to get away with it, just like he and Bay and the others had. Or had they? Everyone else had paid the ultimate price for their sins, and Darek knew that no matter how awful things got, nothing was as bad as he and the other Zodiacs had been.

They pulled up to the house, and Lizzy parked beside the emergency response units that had beaten them there, consisting of one ambulance and two squad cars.

"I hope they haven't touched anything," he said with a sigh.

"They should know better," she said. "But yeah, I hope so too."

They went inside after pushing through the small crowd of neighbors who were beginning to form out on the lawn. Some were trying to stare in the front window.

When Darek walked into Nona's place, he pulled the blinds and turned on a light. Lane was suddenly a lot easier to see. Lizzy walked right over to the body. He didn't look real as he sat on the couch, his mouth a permanent scowl, and his eyes nothing but two large, bloody holes.

Darek walked over and stood next to Bay.

"He deserved better, you know," said Bay quietly. "Out of all of us, he was the one who was the most genuine friend and person."

"Yeah, I liked him too," Darek said. "It's down to the two of us, Bay. I have a feeling that Max isn't going to hold off much longer. He's going to spill his secrets. Our secrets."

Bay leaned in closer. "Don't worry about it, Darek. My plan is almost in motion."

"You found someone to do the deed?" Darek asked. "It's scary how fast some people turn on one another."

"It's a guard," Bay said. "They'll get him from point A to B. He'll look the other way and be unable to stop it. He'll try to pull them away and get knocked out. It's the only way to do it with his reputation intact."

"You've got it all planned out, don't you?" Darek couldn't believe how easy it was for the man to make those kinds of arrangements.

"It's done. All I have to do is give the go ahead, and that's going to come shortly after I see him."

Darek shook his head. "I can't have you go in there and be too obvious. You know people will ask about your sudden interest."

"If that happens, it's my problem," said Bay. "I'll handle it."

"How's Lila?" asked Darek. He was concerned only for the woman and her child. Bay was a controlling asshole who had treated the girl like shit on too many occasions.

"She's huge, complaining, and she's a pain in my ass," he said. "So, she's pretty much normal, aside from missing her sister."

Darek wished she hadn't had to go through that. There had been too many innocent people hurt by all of this. He felt like a selfish ass.

"Have you checked into that lead I gave you?" asked Bay.

Darek knew who he meant. "Stop it," he said. He looked across the room to Lizzy, who raked her hand through her hair and then moved in closer to take some photos. "I have to go help Lizzy with this shit. Don't go anywhere. I'm sure she's going to want to talk to you about things."

"Maybe I'll tell her my suspicions about Raven." Bay met Darek's eyes. "Or at least tell her that Emily's sister might want revenge. She could find out who it is as easy as anyone else."

Darek gave him a hard look. "Maybe we should meet later. You know, after the deed is done. We'll figure out how to flush her out." With that, he walked away, and Bay went to stand by the window, peering out through a crack in the blinds.

Darek walked over to Lizzy, who snapped another photo. A closeup of Lane's sockets. "Did you ask him if he saw anyone coming or going?"

"No, he's just as baffled as us," said Darek. *And talking crazy*, he wanted to add. "What does it look they used for that?" Darek gestured to the holes in Lane's face.

She looked down to the floor. "There's a spoon." She pointed to his foot, where a spoon was left just next to his shoe.

"Jesus. They left the spoon?"

"Yeah," Lizzy said. "I'm sure they got it from the house, but maybe you want to check it out? There's a lot of stuff packed up."

"I'll give it a look." He went to the kitchen but didn't find anything there. When he went back and got a closer look at the pattern on the spoon's handle, something dawned on him. The utensil looked familiar. Too familiar.

"Well?" asked Lizzy.

"No, there are no boxes in there and nothing in the drawers." Because the spoon didn't come from Nona's belongings.

"The team is here, finally," she said, taking a photo of the spoon. "Let's make sure they bag that utensil. I'm hoping there will be prints on it, but let's face it. This asshole is smarter than we're giving them credit for. I want the laptop too. There has to be something on it. I doubt the victim was just casually browsing when this happened, or else the eyes wouldn't have been cut out. Maybe there's a message on it. We'll need to find its charger and take it back to the office once it's been processed. I'll have the computer guys crack into it if it's password protected."

Darek didn't have a good feeling about what was on that computer. If the killer wanted them to find it, it could only mean that there was some type of information linking everything back to him and Bay and what they'd done. He had to make sure that no one else saw the thing. The only way to do that was to make sure it came up missing somehow.

But as soon as forensics came in, Lizzy got with them to collect both items like they were precious. "Make sure these get first attention. I'm sure this isn't our murder weapon, but it should have enough prints on it to royally fuck up someone's life."

Darek thought of what that would mean for him. He didn't want his life totally fucked, royally or otherwise. And if that spoon was from where Darek thought, he better have a damned good excuse.

CHAPTER 26

BAY

Darek and Lizzy were a bit too busy to notice him slipping away, and he couldn't think of a better time to take care of business than the present. He made it all the way to his car without anyone coming after him, so he carefully backed out across the lawn and drove away.

He didn't need to sit around and watch Darek and Lizzy do their thing, and if he needed an alibi, he'd used Lila as an excuse. He had to see Max to get one last word in, and then he was going to make sure the man never saw another sunrise.

He drove across town, hoping Darek wasn't onto him yet. After studying Lane long enough, he'd had time to think, and even though it was brutal and messy, he'd come to the conclusion that a woman might just be capable. It would throw them off, and that was most likely the point.

Bay still couldn't get Raven out of his head, and when he was done with Max, he was going to look for her.

After making it all the way down to the jail without being stopped, he found a parking place and called his friend.

"That was a lot quicker than I expected," said Lawrence.

"Yeah, well, I'm an impatient man. I'm coming up, and I want you to have him waiting for me in room four. Then, after I see him, you'll take him back to the wrong place."

"Can do. I'll need you to keep him busy a minute."

"No problem. And you'll call me back when it's done." Bay had to swing by his office and take care of signing a few paychecks, and he had to gather a few case files if he was going to stay home with Lila. But first, it was time to take care of Max.

He got out of the car, fully intending to be tackled to the ground and arrested. But as he stepped out into the sun, cool wind whipping past him, there wasn't anyone around but a few average citizens going about their day.

He was ready to have his time with the asshole, and when he went inside, he went through the entire process of seeing him, which included signing in, knowing it was going to leave one massive paper trail shortly before Max's demise. But the burden of proof wouldn't be his. He was ready for whatever anyone tried to throw his way.

After waiting nearly half an hour, his phone pinged, and he checked it to see that Darek was looking for him. He didn't bother responding and hoped he had the good sense to cover for him.

Finally, Lawrence called him into the back, "Your client is ready," he said. Bay studied the man's face as he went past him, noticing how calm and collected the man was, even though he was about to do something horrible. *He would have made a good Zodiac.*

Bay would never forget the way Max smiled upon seeing him enter the room, or the feeling of satisfaction he had, knowing the man would soon take his last breath and be left to bleed out on a dirty cell floor.

"I wondered when you'd get your turn," Max said. "Every dog has his day. Isn't that the old saying?"

"I'd say that's appropriate in your case," said Bay.

"I heard you found Mia. How was she? Did she ask about me?"

"You hoped I'd be there, didn't you?" Bay asked. "That's why you didn't tell anyone sooner. You hoped that Darek and I would find Mia, and it would all play out just how you wanted."

"I think it *has* worked out the way I wanted it to. But tell me, did you get to see the life drain from her eyes?"

Bay tried to maintain his composure, so he turned off his hate and made sure he didn't show it. "Yeah, I did. I have to give you credit. It was clever the way you did it."

"Thank you. I mean, I don't want to brag."

"Nor should you. I mean, we know you had help. I just wonder how that bitch had the stomach to pull it off. I mean, a fucking woman? She'd have to be a ruthless bitch to do something like that."

Max's eyes lit with surprise. "You know about her, do you?"

"Yeah, and I'd say she's my kind of woman."

Max grinned. "She'd kill you for saying that."

"Ah, that's right," Bay said. "She hates me. I forgot for a minute about that. I mean, it's all about revenge, right? You for your father? Her for her sister?"

"You're the one who knows so fucking much all of a sudden. You tell me." He rattled his cuffs and adjusted in his seat to lean in closer. "I can tell you this. You're going to pay your price as well. You all will. Even Darek Blake isn't safe."

"He's your old friend, isn't he? Man, you're so clever to play him like you did. As far as Darek, I can't speak for him, but I fully intend to get my revenge for all of my men. Each and every one of them."

"Even the ones *you* killed?" asked Max. "You pretend to be the victim, but I know. I know how many of them died at your hand."

Bay was not rattled. Everything he had done was necessary. "You know a lot, too, don't you?" Bay leaned in closer. "I appreciate you keeping your silence."

"I'll tell all when the time is right."

"When *she* tells you, you mean?" Bay hoped to rile him up. "You see, I have a theory. I think *she* runs the show. Tell me I'm wrong."

Max's eyes narrowed, and he clammed up as his mouth turned down in a frown.

Bay knew he had him. He'd accomplished what he wanted to, and now he could go. He got up and gave Max one last look. The piece of shit was going to get everything he deserved.

He had already made sure the other men were in place, and now the guard would lead him to his doom. Bay only wished he could see it, or better yet, that he could do it himself. He walked out of the room and gave Lawrence a nod.

As he walked out, he heard Max screaming. "Get back here, Collins! You sorry motherfucker! You're going to pay!"

Bay kept walking, knowing it was all going to play out perfectly, with Max acting out. He calmly walked out of the building, making sure to sign out and not caring what that could mean. He walked to his car, thinking about Mia. She had been so scared the last few moments of her life, and now, he hoped that Max would have that same fear when he realized what would happen to him.

Bay went out to his car, hoping he'd soon have a call, but first, he had to go to his office and take care of some things before the end of the workday. He had been so busy with Mia and Lila that he had called to take a bit of time before his next big trial. Luckily, the case was not for another two months, and he would be ready and on his A-game when the time came. He'd have Mia's ashes scattered by then, and Lila would be doing better and closer to delivering his son.

His son. He'd really gotten lucky with Lila. Maybe he had picked the right sister all along, but he wasn't sure he believed in that "meant to be" bullshit anyway. Things were the way they were because of choices, and he would always take ownership of his decisions.

He pulled up at his office building and found his usual parking space, which was reserved just for him, and then went inside.

As always, he was greeted by his receptionist. "Good afternoon, Mr. Collins."

He gave a nod and kept walking, making his way to the elevator. When he got inside, he leaned against the railing, which he never did, and one thought of his son had him standing firmly on two feet again. He had to remain strong, and he had come too far to falter with who he was.

He went straight to his desk, and as he settled in, he called downstairs for the checks to be sent up. Then he reached into his desk for his pen case and froze. The damned drawer was still full of Mia's panties, and he stopped for a moment and looked at them. Then he pushed the drawer shut, not ready to get rid of them.

There was a knock on his door. "Mr. Collins?"

"Yes," he said, "I'll take those over here." He wasn't going to get up to get them, and the girl looked so afraid to come any closer. He hadn't seen her before. "You're new?"

"Yes, sir. I'm down in the accounting department." The girl had big doe eyes and golden blonde hair that wasn't quite the same color as Mia's but very flattering to her complexion.

"Don't bother being nervous. You're welcome anytime." He liked what he saw. The woman was not only pretty, but she had a nice sense of style and a love of short skirts, just like Mia.

"Thank you." She pulled a stray strand of hair behind her ear and gave him a shy smile as she walked into the room and placed the stack of checks on his desk. "Do you want me to wait while you sign them?"

"Yeah, that's fine. You could make yourself comfortable if you want." He put his hand on the small of her back. "The couch is quite soft." He wondered how hard it would be to groom her. He would miss Mia being at work with him, and maybe this girl could take her place and fill that void.

He took his time signing his name and watched the girl closely. "What's your name?" he asked as he signed the last check.

"Marlena." She met his eyes with another smile, and he got up and walked over to her.

"Well, here you go, Marlena. Feel free to pop in anytime and use my couch." He handed her the checks, and she got to her feet.

"Thank you, Mr. Collins."

"Please, call me Bay." As he extended his hand, he noticed a blinking light over her shoulder at the fax machine. He wanted to flirt, but he remembered the text and wondered if Kenneth Warner had ever sent anything over.

"Thank you, Bay. That's a beautiful name." She turned and headed toward the door. "I'll take you up on that."

As she left, Bay walked over and checked the machine. He took the stack of papers from the tray and thumbed through them. Mixed in with all the paperwork was a black and white photograph. The picture of a young girl, a dark-haired beauty who Bay recognized.

A slow smile spread his lips. "You sneaky fucking bitch."

To be continued...

ABOUT THE AUTHOR

WL Knightly is a thriller/murder mystery co-writing pen name for USA Today Best Selling Authors Lexy Timms and Ali Parker.

When she's not writing, Lexy can be found dealing in Antique Jewelry and hanging out with her awesome hubby and three kids.

Ali is a CPA turned fiction writer who is married to her best friend and lives in Texas. She spends her days writing and chasing three kiddos around the house.

The two friends met years ago when they both started writing and publishing in various young adult genres and needed a critique partner. The rest is history...

Made in the USA
Coppell, TX
17 July 2021

59086326R00089